BY LARISSA PHAM

Pop Song: Adventures in Art and Intimacy

Discipline

DISCIPLINE

DISCIPLINE

A Novel

LARISSA PHAM

RANDOM HOUSE

New York

Random House
An imprint and division of Penguin Random House LLC
1745 Broadway, New York, NY 10019
randomhousebooks.com
penguinrandomhouse.com

LIBRARY OF CONGRESS CATALOGING-IN-PUBLICATION DATA
Names: Pham, Larissa author
Title: Discipline: a novel / Larissa Pham.
Description: New York, NY: Random House, 2026.
Identifiers: LCCN 2025030421 (print) | LCCN 2025030422 (ebook) | ISBN 9780593979648 hardcover | ISBN 9780593979655 ebook
Subjects: LCSH: Novelists—Fiction | Teacher-student relationships—Fiction | LCGFT: Psychological fiction | Novels
Classification: LCC PS3616.H358 D57 2026 (print) | LCC PS3616.H358 (ebook) | DDC 813/.6—dc23/eng/20250715
LC record available at https://lccn.loc.gov/2025030421
LC ebook record available at https://lccn.loc.gov/2025030422

Printed in the United States of America

1st Printing

First Edition

BOOK TEAM: Production editor: Cara DuBois · Managing editor: Rebecca Berlant · Production manager: Katie Zilberman · Proofreaders: Julie Ehlers, Alissa Fitzgerald

Book design by Debbie Glasserman

The authorized representative in the EU for product safety and compliance is Penguin Random House Ireland, Morrison Chambers, 32 Nassau Street, Dublin D02 YH68, Ireland. https://eu-contact.penguin.ie

A woman must continually watch herself. She is almost continually accompanied by her own image of herself.

JOHN BERGER, *Ways of Seeing*

though it may look like (*Write* it!) like disaster.

ELIZABETH BISHOP, "One Art"

CONTENTS

I

The artist works. Here is her domain. Her brushes, paints, knives, and pigments. The metal surface of her worktable wiped clean. Here is her canvas, bare and stretched. Four perfect corners. The fabric is ready, the tooth eagerly raised: She glides her fingers across it. Drums against the taut fabric that refuses to give. She applies the gesso with a wide, flat brush. White medium flowing over the canvas. Broad, slow strokes until the surface is filled. The canvas now shining. The canvas blank. She waits.

CELMINS

⸺

I was running late, and by the time I got to the gate they were asking people to check their bags because the overhead compartments were full. I was late because I love being in airports—that floating, anonymous feeling—and I had lingered too long at a café, thinking I had arrived early enough to sit with a coffee. I hadn't, so on the jet bridge I turned over my suitcase and boarded the plane.

After we landed, I went to the baggage claim and stood, waiting, for thirty minutes until I realized someone else had taken my bag. There was a black hard-shell suitcase going around on the belt but it wasn't mine, and I felt a sudden lightness, a disorientation. By this point I was late again, so after talking to the airline, I took the elevated train to just north of the city, where I was giving a reading at a university. While I was on the train, my phone rang.

The person who took your bag called to let us know they have it, the airline representative said. He's offering to return it to you, or he can bring it to the airport and you can pick it up there.

I'm fine with meeting him, I said. I pressed a fingertip against my free ear to block out the noise of the train.

I gave the representative permission to share my phone number and stepped onto the exposed platform. A hard wind was blowing over the water. When I turned to look at the shore, a few blocks in the distance, I knew it was a lake, but it extended so far into the horizon it seemed like the ocean. Because it was freshwater, the tides were smaller, I assumed, and posed less of a danger to construction, and so the city was built right up to its edge. That seemed wrong to me. The city felt perched on the lip of nothingness, a settlement on the bank of infinity.

The reading was in a handsome Gothic building set on the quad. It was the first stop on my book tour—I used *tour* euphemistically, usually when talking to strangers or acquaintances about my trip. I had written a novel, my first, and it had been published by a small press in the spring. Shortly before the book was to come out, my relationship of five years ended. Then I had wanted nothing more than to leave my own life. By cobbling together speaking fees from universities, which had recently reopened to in-person events, and relying on the goodwill of friends here and there for a place to stay, I was able to plan a loose itinerary, moving in stops across the country. I had never traveled through America like this. After my ex moved out, I busied myself with booking events and finding a subletter for the time I would be away from our apartment, which was now solely my apartment, and which I could not afford on my own. This was an issue, I knew, that would become only more pressing with time, but with the month's rent secured and a subletter installed, I packed my suitcase and departed.

The reading went well. I read from a scene early in the book, the one I had decided I would read at all my events, a scene where the artist is in her studio, waiting for something or someone to arrive. Then I gave a short talk. After, there was a question and answer session with the professor who had invited me to campus, and then the discussion opened up to the students. Though I was still relatively new to the business of being a working writer, I liked speaking at schools—the Q&A always seemed more lively, with higher stakes. I liked seeing the serious faces of the students as they listened, and I liked the way they asked questions that were nearly exclusively occupied with the structures of their own lives. There was something sweet about their solipsism, to witness how visibly they were constructing their convictions, which after this interval might remain in place for years.

Near the end of the event, a student in the front row raised her hand and waited for the mic to come her way. A tiny silver cross glittered at her throat.

When you write, do you have a plan? she asked. Or do you see it as an act of faith?

I wasn't sure how to answer.

I usually start with a plan, I said. A scenario I want to explore, some kind of relationship or tension I'm interested in, something that provokes the initial impulse. But once I begin writing, things start to change.

She nodded, waiting for me.

So I suppose you could say from that point on it's an act of faith, I said. I do have to have faith in the characters to tell me what to do, and I have to have faith in my own ability to tell a story. But it's possible I have a different idea of faith than you do.

Other students had remained seated as they spoke, but this student had chosen to stand. She wore her hair in two puffs high on either side of her head, and they bobbed gently as she nodded, listening. I see, she said. Maybe it's not so different. In a way, you're trusting that the story inside you will come out in the way that it's intended. Right?

Well, I said. Sometimes I feel more like a conduit for it. At a point, it starts to take over, and I have to listen.

A beautiful expression moved across her face.

I've felt that way before, she said. Sometimes, I feel the story in my body. It begins somewhere in my heart and moves all the way down to my hands . . .

She held one out now and flexed it, her painted nails flashing in the low light of the auditorium. And it builds and it builds, and—once, she said, gripping the mic with both hands now, once, I was at work, and a story came to me, nearly in its entirety. And I couldn't write it down—I had to let it build, this tremendous pressure, ratcheting up and up and up until my shift ended and on the train home I typed it all on my phone, my fingers flying, not looking up until it was finished.

She fell silent, waiting for me to respond. Someone in the audience shifted, as if to release the pressure she had invoked. A restlessness moved through the crowd. In the front row, I saw a woman shake out her hands and reach into her bag.

But it doesn't happen all the time, the student said. How do you—when that doesn't happen. How do you know when something is worth working on?

I remembered being her age. Earnest to a fault, so certain of art's power and possibility. I too had once believed I had special talent, that there existed something only I could make, and that I deserved to make it. The student's face shone with a lovely, milky opacity. I wanted her to keep believing this—that she was capable of great things. But I couldn't think of anything to say in the moment that wouldn't sound bald and false.

You don't, I said. You don't know whether something is worth continuing, not until you've started it. And sometimes even then you don't know. But you have to keep working at it, I said.

I was using a microphone too, one clipped to the collar of my shirt. My voice sounded tinny and unfamiliar, lagging slightly through the auditorium speakers, and for a moment, I wasn't sure if it was actually me speaking. It seemed like the voice of someone else.

When you were writing this book, the student said, how did you know?

I didn't, I said. But I had to write it.

How many times had I thought this, said it to myself and others. I had to write it. There was no alternative, no world in which I hadn't.

After the event there was a short reception, and by the time things were winding down it was around three in the afternoon. I had been awake since the very early morning. As part of the speaking invitation the university had booked me a room in a hotel downtown; though perhaps it was too much effort for one day, I'd intended to visit a museum, too. But there was still the matter of my missing suitcase, and I lingered at the entrance to the university building, considering what to do next. In an alcove, next to benches where I supposed students gathered between classes, there was an array of flyers and postcards—advertisements for talks and cultural events. I sat on a bench and flipped through a stack of flyers, phone in hand. A well-known poet was giving a talk in two weeks; looking at the dates, I had just missed the An-My Lê show at the Museum of Contemporary Photography. Then I saw on one postcard a painting I knew. Or rather, I knew the painter.

My phone rang and I answered it. With my free hand I turned the postcard over so the image was no longer visible.

Hi, said a man's voice. Is this Christine?

Yes, I said.

Hi, uh, I have your bag.

Oh, good.

I'm so sorry, he said. He sounded embarrassed, young. This has never happened to me before. Uh, I don't know where you are, but I could meet you in the Loop, if that's convenient for you. Downtown, I mean.

Don't worry about it, I said. That's fine for me. I was actually planning to stop by the Art Institute, so maybe you could meet me there.

On it, he said, his voice swelling with relief. I'm going so fast, I'm already there. I've got your bag, I'm waiting for you. I'm sitting on the steps. Man, it's nice out today.

I laughed in spite of myself. It's okay, I said. I turned the postcard back, looked at the painting. Abstract. Slashes of violet bleeding over dull gray, a smear of acid green. Then I set it down again. Really, I said. I'll be there in an hour.

The man who had my bag was a redheaded graduate student in his third year studying cellular and molecular biology. I learned all this as we stood on the steps of the museum, talking in the sun. He looked a few years younger than me, lanky as if he'd grown very quickly while still a child, with ruddy cheeks and freckles in a spray across his nose and forehead. We didn't seem to have much in common aside from our taste in suitcases. His hand still rested lightly on the handle of mine, his knuckles red, too.

I can take that, I said.

Oh, god. Yes, take it away from me before I run off with it again, he said. I slid it toward me on the steps until the wheels bumped against my shoes.

What brings you to the city? he asked. Or are you just passing through?

I'm here for two days, I said, and told him about my event at the university.

That's great, he said. It sounds like people are actually interested when you talk at them. I'm not so lucky. At science conferences, even the scientists get bored.

What are you researching? I asked him.

It's a little complicated, he said. You really want to know?

Sure, I said.

So I'm researching molecular biology as it relates to cell development, he said. In the early stages of cell development, there are a few things, a few variables that affect how the cell develops, which affects the organism in turn.

What kind of variables?

Well, take symmetry, for example. You know how humans have two of everything, arms, legs, to a point. One heart. One brain. That's bilateral symmetry.

Okay, I said.

Right, so we have all these animals and organisms that develop bilateral symmetry on the outside. But their internal organs, those aren't symmetrical. So sometimes, some organisms don't develop the way they're supposed to. Like maybe you get an animal with an extra-big heart because it's doubled when it shouldn't be.

Sure, I said.

So what I do is . . . well, so someone else figures out why things like that happen. Haha, sorry, I guess that was kind of misleading. So someone figures out the very small changes, very small environmental conditions, that affect those early stages of an organism's development. But what I specifically do is try to figure out how the parts of the cell are talking to each other in that moment, on a molecular level.

Talking to each other? I asked.

Right, like . . .

I watched as he pursed his lips, thinking. They were thin, chapped and pale.

Like, they're not really talking to each other, he said. Not like you and I are talking. It's more like a series of alerts that get fired off that tell different components what to do. How do I put it . . . it's how decisions get made in the presence of stimuli. But they're not really decisions, they don't have minds. They're like—signals.

Signals, I said.

Yeah. Signals without words, without speech, that tell them what to do. He chewed on his lip. Man, I don't know if I explained it right. Sorry I've been talking for so long. You're a great listener.

Thanks, I said. I really was curious, so don't worry.

We stood on the steps. The afternoon sun glared off the limestone and the bronze lions on either side of us. He shaded his eyes with one hand.

Were you going to go to the museum? he asked.

Yes, I said, I'd meant to.

Well, hey, he said. I wasn't going to go back to the airport until later anyway. Would you mind if I joined you?

His name was Henry. I left my suitcase at the coat check and we decided to see the contemporary exhibit on view. As we walked up the marble staircase of the museum, he asked about my novel.

So it's a book about art?

I had told him that I had just given a talk about writing inspired by visual art and archives, but that didn't really summarize what the book was about, or why I had written it.

It's more like a book about an artist, I said. I thought about what to say next. Who becomes entangled in an affair with an older painter, I said.

Oh, he said.

Which ends badly.

I'm sorry.

Don't be sorry, I said. It's fiction.

He nodded.

You could call it a revenge fantasy, actually.

He nodded again, looking uncertain.

I'm not an artist, I said.

Henry turned to look at me. Under the bright lights of the museum, his eyes were pale green, like the first few feet of water at a beach.

No, he said. You're an author. Hey, can I ask a stupid question?

He didn't wait for me to answer.

Sometimes I read a book, and it really seems like everything's true, the way the person's writing and everything, but it's supposed to be a novel. Does that happen often, or am I just bad at reading?

We walked through a long, rectangular gallery displaying Indian and Southeast Asian art, mostly religious sculpture. It was one of those parts of a museum that feel historical, nearly anthropological. I was always a little disconcerted by the ancient, primordial aura that seemed to emanate from those kinds of exhibits, as if time itself had stopped. Identity then seemed like something fixed in stone, like a carved Buddha, with long, wise earlobes that would never move, never be pressed against a shoulder or stroked gently by a loving hand.

When I was still with my ex, when I couldn't sleep, I'd reach over and stroke his earlobes, feeling soothed. Sometimes he woke, but usually he kept sleeping.

It probably happens more often than we'd expect, I said. People are always writing from their own lives, and it sneaks into the text, even if we think we're making things up. But there are also people who write books based on their lives and just change the names. Or, well, sometimes they don't even change the names, they just keep them in.

Then what's the point? Henry asked, stopping beside me. If I wrote novels, I'd make up stuff all the time.

I was looking at a small, jade-colored teacup on a saucer, presented in a vitrine. The cup had a narrowed foot on which it stood, elevating it slightly, and both cup and plate had frilled edges. The glaze was layered, with an underpainting, which gave the pieces an organic look, like they had been made of leaves. Looking at domestic objects in museums always made me weirdly emotional. I imagined the tea the cup once held, the long-dead mouth that would have pressed to its rim.

Some people write to make sense of what they've experienced, I said. I turned from the vitrine and began walking again, and Henry moved to keep pace. Or maybe they think life is an interesting story, I said, one worth referring back to. You can't ever change what's already happened to you, but when you write about it, you can at least reframe it. Take control of it, maybe.

That's fair, he said.

We entered the modern wing of the museum, where natural light spilled in through tall glass windows.

I took a poetry workshop once, he said. In college.

How was it?

I liked it, he said. The writing, I mean. But I never listened to any workshop feedback. I hardly ever revised, actually. By the time the poem had been read by someone else, it had completely changed states. States of matter, like from solid to gas. Or maybe the other way around—the poems I thought had something special felt so dead after class. It was like they had been beheaded. I couldn't imagine going back to edit them. It would be like—like editing a tumbleweed.

What kind of poems did you write? I asked.

That's the thing, he said. I thought I was going to write about all kinds of lofty subjects. But I ended up writing the dumbest stuff . . . little things from my life, mostly. Anxiety about the girl I was dating. It was fun, but I stopped writing after the class was over. I guess I was kind of disappointed I hadn't tried to reach further outside of my own life.

There was a group of tourists moving slowly through the special exhibit, following an audio guide on their phones. We waited to let them pass, and they gathered around a large, moody abstract painting, jagged dark shapes hovering over mountainous silhouettes in browns and yellows. They stood in a semicircle in front of it, faces tilted up. While Henry had been speaking, I'd let my gaze wander freely around the room, observing the other people and the curation of the work on the walls. The show had been billed as a reimagining and exploration of contemporary art, which in reality meant that it was mostly abstract, mostly large works from male artists who had first achieved fame in the 1960s. Now, as Henry stopped to look at a painting, I stopped to watch him looking.

Ever since I'd moved to New York I had liked going to shows with friends and acquaintances. I liked the ritual of it: meeting outside the subway on a weekend morning, huddling over our phones to decide what we'd see. It was a way to talk without talking, to be together and separate at the same time. I found, too, that it was a good way to get to know someone—that the way someone moved through a show often disclosed who they were, and what they cared to pay attention to.

When I was young, I made aesthetic judgments quickly, deciding after a few seconds if I liked or disliked something. I was like that with art, with books, and with people. But in my adulthood I found myself lingering longer and longer in front of things, even work I didn't like at first, standing very still in front of each piece, always reading the wall text.

I knew I was slow in this way; I couldn't help it. My ex had preferred to walk through a gallery quickly, catalog in hand, scanning the text for highlighted works, which he would look at first, wanting to grasp the overarching concept of an exhibition. He would pace multiple laps around a gallery before I had even completed one, and in the beginning of our relationship this distracted me—feeling him move close, then away. For him, all looking required a hierarchy: He had to know what was worth paying attention to, and what wasn't. But I found that I needed to pay attention to everything in order to understand what really was important.

By the end of our relationship, when we went to museums together, I always lost him, my last sight of him his back as he disappeared into another, farther room. We'd meet again on the ground floor, in the lobby or gift shop. Then we'd debrief together, hands in our pockets, our mouths full of judgments and phrases, and I did enjoy those moments. Even though we were never separated for very long it felt like a reunion, as if, armed with the disparate experiences of having seen something, we were able to, however briefly, become new to each other again.

Henry, I noticed, was a restless gallerygoer. His eyes drifted around the canvas, lit on the wall text, went back to the picture. Because I was standing still, he stayed beside me, but I could feel him waiting for me to say something. Eventually he spoke.

What do you think of this one?

We were standing in front of a small, compact oil painting; I recognized it as a Vija Celmins, and was surprised to see her work in the exhibition. The painting was on a wooden panel, which stood out about an inch from the wall, and its surface was very smooth. The canvas was entirely filled with ocean waves, without a horizon line. They seemed nearly photorealistic, but I could tell from the slightly matte finish and the suggestion of brushstrokes that they were painted. The work had that glow peculiar to layered oils—as if it were lit from within. I liked the piece, and told Henry as much. I was usually drawn to images that had no distinct focal point; they let the eye rove around. And I liked the waves, which were in motion, choppy and with foamy peaks.

I like it too, but it seems a little boring, he said. I don't get why it's not a photograph.

I like that it's not a photograph, I said. It took time to make. A photo would be too easy, don't you think?

Well, yeah, he said. Either you or I could do that.

Is there a painting here you like better? I asked, and he pointed to the Clyfford Still, where the tourists had gathered. They were in the next room now; I could see one of them through the doorway, face obscured by a wide-brimmed hat.

I like the drama of it, he said. The peaks, the irregular shapes. It's not something I would have come up with. And it's big.

Sure, I said, I like that one too.

I think maybe I just don't like things that seem too close to life, he said. If I'm going to look at something someone else made, I really want it to surprise me.

I understood that. Life was all around us, all the time. Sometimes, I thought, it felt like there was too much life to handle—too much detail, all crammed into reality, from which we could rarely escape. There was no filter, no strategic compression of narrative through which we could fast-forward—just the onslaught of each moment and its accompanying sensation. Lately I had found myself overwhelmed by the sheer density of the Northeast, by the thicket of memories it held; that was part of why I had decided to go on this trip. I didn't tell Henry all this, but I did tell him I understood what he meant.

We walked through the rest of the special exhibit together, talking. It turned out that Henry wasn't much for fine art, but he loved movies, particularly noir and thrillers. It was their slight but exaggerated distance from reality that he enjoyed. He knew from the first minute of a noir film that it was a noir, and the same with a thriller. From there it was easy to sit back and enjoy the inevitably convoluted, coincidence-filled storylines that nevertheless kept him interested until the very end. It was hard to make something that felt true to life, so why bother? He preferred when a movie told you exactly what it was from the start.

There was something about genre, I agreed, that made it more fun to participate in. It was as though once you knew the rules and conventions, you could see how a film was in dialogue with them. When a movie was confused about what it was, it became harder to appreciate; it was as though you didn't know what game you were playing, and were therefore unable to keep score. But I still found myself drawn to realism, which perhaps was a genre of its own, with its own conventions. By replicating life, were we able to say something new about it?

When I had first encountered Celmins, it was the craft of her work that I found alluring. Almost entirely by chance I had walked into an exhibition of her prints, a satellite show to a retrospective happening at a major museum uptown. The prints, mostly aquatints and woodcuts, were mesmerizing—soft, shallow strokes that carved out the shapes of ocean waves, not at the point of breaking but as they appeared miles from the coastline. That part of the ocean, static as it seemed, was constantly changing, minute to minute. But in her prints it stayed the same: caught in that frozen moment for as long as the paper held. I wanted to know if it was memory or nostalgia that kept her there, making images of a single instant.

Why, I asked Henry, if he didn't really care for fine art, had he decided to come to the museum?

Well, he said. It's really nice out today. I didn't want to go back to O'Hare right away, and because I don't have any of my stuff, I couldn't really go back to campus. See—I just got back from visiting my girlfriend. Normally I'd be getting back into research, going to the lab, trying to catch up. But right now, thanks to my suitcase mix-up, I don't have anywhere to be, I don't have anything to do, I don't have any responsibilities.

I asked if he had been visiting the same girlfriend from his poems.

He laughed then, and his face got red. No, no, he said. That was a different girl. Man, that's embarrassing to think about. Those poems . . . no, Aya and I broke up that spring. She was a year ahead of me and moving to San Francisco to work in tech after graduation. Maybe we could have stayed together, but, I dunno. I doubt it. He looked at me sheepishly.

After we broke up, I didn't know what to do, he said. I had all this writing about her. So I stuck all my poems into a zip file where I'd never see them, and I printed out our emails and then deleted them.

He understood that that sounded strange—printing out emails. But they used to write to each other, he explained. They had been seeing each other, very casually, before Aya left for a summer fellowship abroad. The night before her flight, feeling the pang of oncoming separation, they had dropped into an abrupt intimacy. He drove her to the airport, and as she was stepping out of the car, she said: I'll write to you.

Have you ever written a love letter? Henry asked, though again he didn't wait for my response. Their letters—he had never thought of himself as a writer, and his failures in poetry workshop probably proved he wasn't, but he had loved writing to Aya. It had cast his quotidian life in the lab into a new, sunnier light, every detail illumined by the mythology of their correspondence. Meanwhile, in long, charmingly meandering emails, she shared with him her insecurities and anxieties, her dream of becoming a playwright. With each missive they exchanged, their longing for each other deepened, and though they'd been sleeping together for months, it felt as though now, for the first time, they were truly able to communicate.

When she returned to campus in the fall they circled each other warily at first. It seemed impossible that they could return to the casual sexual relationship they had established before. But then they realized they didn't have to. They had already laid everything out in their letters; now they only had to trust each other to follow the plot. There was an awkwardness to their initial reconnection: They had never before gone to dinner; they had never been to the movies. Still, they started dating in earnest.

She hadn't wanted to work in tech, he explained; her true passion was theater. But by the spring, around the time of his poetry class, Aya had been grappling with the fact that her life outside of school would look different from the future she had imagined for herself. She started applying for corporate jobs, ones that seemed to have nothing to do with her interests or beliefs, and Henry noticed she began cooling toward him, too.

When an offer came from a big tech company, she took it, even though it required moving across the country. That was when their relationship ended—not, Henry now understood, because of the distance, but because she had chosen something that made her a fundamentally different person from whom she had been when they first started dating. Not a bad person, he was quick to say. But a different person.

He was certain she was happy now; the position she'd taken allowed her to live well, and her Instagram—he still checked on her, sometimes—was mostly photos of meals at nice restaurants. She seemed to travel a lot. She never posted pictures of herself.

I sensed that Henry was upset with Aya for not staying true to what he believed was her self. Perhaps he had fallen in love with what he thought of as the truest, most authentic version of her, and when her priorities shifted, he saw that as a betrayal of some kind. But maybe it was the case that her priorities had always been one way— a pleasant life, financial stability—and her choices at the end of college only served to illuminate the differences between them, and indeed the different options available to each of them. It seemed entirely possible to me that Aya had done what was best for herself, or at least what she thought was necessary for her to live a good life.

It sounds like it was a difficult breakup, I said.

Yeah, it was. It really sucked. But what's crazy is that my girl-friend now lives in San Francisco, too. It's been going for about a year, we met here and she moved. I wasn't trying to be in a long-distance relationship . . . He paused, hand on the nape of his neck. He pulled at the hair there, like it had something to tell him.

So I've been flying to California, he said. And every time I'm there, even though I'm dating someone else now, I think I'm going to run into Aya. In fact, I kind of hope I do. I don't know what I'd do if I saw her again. I don't even know what she's really like anymore. Maybe she's changed to the point that I wouldn't recognize her. But I'm always glancing at every girl on the street, wondering if it's her.

We had looped back to the original entrance so I could get my suitcase, and we stood under the Beaux Arts ceiling, so different from the light and glass of the modern wing where we had just been. It felt dark inside, and cramped. Henry pushed the doors open for me and I stepped through. Outside, the sun was setting. I was hungry. I was looking forward to getting to the hotel, to having a seat at the bar and ordering something for dinner. A steak, maybe. Or a burger. The kind of thing people ate away from home—meat that bled.

Thanks for joining me, I said. I tugged my suitcase down the first step. And for bringing this back.

No, thanks for letting me come with you, he said.

In the softening light, his eyes looked more hazel than green. Then he leaned toward me and inclined his head slightly and I stood very still, so that he would understand that I didn't want to kiss him.

I put both hands on the handle of my bag. I'm going to go, I said.

Sorry, he said. I'm really sorry. I must have misread—

You didn't read anything, I said.

I left him on the steps, his hands empty, his mouth slightly open. I wondered where his thoughts were leading him in that moment. If they were taking him to San Francisco, where Aya was, if he was wandering the streets in his head even now, looking for her.

Walking to the station for the elevated rail, I stopped at the bottom of the stairs for a moment before deciding to walk on to the hotel. The streets were full of people rushing home, their heads down, and I wanted to disappear into the crowd.

I had been surprised to encounter the Celmins painting, surprised at what that encounter stirred in me. After seeing her prints I had gone to her retrospective at the museum uptown, where I spent a long time in front of one object, a vitrine containing rocks and pebbles arranged on a white base. At first glance the rocks seemed randomly selected, dull enough that one's eyes could flick across them without noticing anything. But each rock actually had a duplicate, a twin that had been cast in bronze and painted. Some were placed side by side with the original, prompting a comparison; other pairs lay on opposite sides of the plinth, the separation making them more eerie, as though the identicals had been found, not manufactured. Each fleck of color, each ridge and texture on the original rocks—which had been found in the New Mexico desert, the placard explained—had been painstakingly replicated by the artist.

After the show, I'd read a review of it that disparaged the painted rocks, arguing that as a gimmick, they invited only something as simple as a technical comparison. The reviewer had preferred Celmins's earlier paintings, which seemed to evoke her childhood as a refugee at the end of the Second World War. I sensed that the critic had wanted Celmins to make work with a legible story behind it, work that spoke directly to her lived experience of trauma. But I found myself drawn to the rocks, not only for their technical precision but for the way they seemed to invert the relationship between life and art—for how they forced us to consider all the coincidence and causation that went into the creation of something we didn't consider created, something as ordinary and humble as a stone.

Maybe it was true that Celmins's desire to fix the image in memory bordered on maniacal. Her work had a fine-grained, virtuosic realism, a total surrender to the pure image that could only be the result of time and labor, a quality I had always admired in the work of others and never managed to achieve myself. I had never had the patience, wanting the image now, now, now. I had lied to Henry when I told him I wasn't an artist, though it was true that I wasn't anymore: I had left that discipline. But I had been once, or to be more accurate, I believed I could have been.

I thought of what he said about how organisms developed symmetry. I had always taken my own for granted, my two arms and two legs, my ten fingers and ten toes. I looked at my own hands now, white and ghostly in the depleting light. It was strange to think that one small condition, before I was conscious of it, or even capable of consciousness, had led to all this, making me the shape I was shaped.

I had never truly tried to replicate life the way Celmins did, in its exactitude, down to the finest detail. But I did think there was something important, maybe even necessary, in trying to make something that depicted, even if not life as it was, then life as how it felt.

———

The hotel was old and elegant. Tall ceilings, dark wood. When I arrived, the man at the front desk said, with some confusion, that it seemed I had already checked in, a room was already occupied under my name, and given the long, strange doubling of the day I wondered if I really had come by earlier, if I was forgetting something I shouldn't forget, but it was soon sorted. An error in the system, he said.

After having dinner at the bar, I went back upstairs and showered and changed into more comfortable clothes. I left my room and walked outside, to where the lake met the city. There was a beach, small and sandy—I hadn't thought there would be sand. My feet sank with each step, and eventually I stooped to take off my shoes, carrying them in one hand. It was night. Trees framed the horizon, which, in the dark, began to merge with the lake. I stood at the edge of the shore and looked east. The water went on for so long, and there was nothing at the end of it—nothing that I could see.

He sees her at first from a distance. Her hair a dark shape in the corridor. She is carrying something bulky under her arm, a long bundle of wooden stretcher bars. She walks steadily: Her footsteps echo down the hall. Where is she going? The freight elevator. The painting studios are on the third floor. If he leaves now, he may catch her. He hesitates. Then follows.

HOPPER

I had planned to take a bus to the next stop on my tour, a small liberal arts school a few hours west, but at the last minute the college told me that a professor from another department was driving back from the city and would be able to give me a ride. It might be more pleasant, the department chair said. At noon I arrived at Union Station, where a woman stood, hands loosely clasped, face tilted toward the sun. I knew she was the person I was looking for and that I should go to her, but instead of quickening my stride I slowed down, until I was walking like I lived there and had nowhere in particular to be. She wore her long hair in small, dark braids and was dressed simply, in black jeans and a gray T-shirt, and she carried a tote bag bearing the logo of a local literary magazine. I was surprised she wasn't reading, or looking at her phone, and it made me wonder what kind of person

she was, and how long she had been waiting for me like this. When
she heard me approach she turned and smiled.

Zoë? I said, and she nodded.

It's nice to meet you, she said, her voice mellifluous. I'm parked
just this way.

We drove out of the city, avoiding most of the traffic. Zoë turned on
the radio with one hand, scanning for a classical station, she said, and
I asked her what she taught.

I'm in queer studies, she answered, her eyes still on the road. My
research area is, broadly, the internet. How it creates new kinds of
communities, especially around identity. But what's interesting, she
added, glancing at me, is that I've been learning so much from my
students. I'm not the only expert in the room.

How so? I asked.

The internet's constantly changing, she said. When I started my
PhD, I felt like I was part of the groups I was researching. A lot of my
academic writing had this flavor of—

She paused, tapping two fingers on the steering wheel along to the
beat of a concerto that was playing at low volume.

—Of confession, she said, or first-person experience; it colored
everything. The introductions to my papers were always personal,
she continued. Which made sense. I was talking about identity poli-
tics, marginalization, the formation of self through internet culture.
For a while no one was really writing about it, certainly not while I
was beginning my dissertation, and I felt like I had to. But now—I'm
older, and more settled in my offline identity. I'm not part of those
in-groups anymore, and new pockets of online culture have formed
that are inaccessible to me. I wouldn't even know where to begin to

find them, nor would I be able to participate, not authentically. It's fascinating.

What kind of pockets? I asked her.

Like— Her mouth quirked up in a smile, and I was surprised by how cool and level even that expression was. I had thought my question might break her into warmth, but there was something inaccessible about her. It's sweet, actually, she said. Do you know anything about role-play? Online?

No, I said. I don't think so.

I asked her to explain it to me and she spoke while she drove. The road was flat and on either side of us rose tall stands of corn, and in flashes of yellow, sunflower fields. It was a new thing young people did, she said, maybe not just young people, almost certainly not just young people, but they were the ones telling her about it. They pretended to be other people, online, playing characters whom they created and who existed in worlds that they built. The characters they role-played even had relationships together, ones that could mirror or diverge from the relationships of their real-life lives, and it was, she said, very emotional for some of them. This role-playing. There was so much that could be altered from one's ordinary life, refashioned into a character. You could have a new name, a new gender; you didn't even have to be fully human if being human didn't feel right. She thought the internet was perhaps a place where, with different names, even bodies, her students could work out the problems of their real-world lives.

While Zoë talked, I imagined building a glass staircase. This was how I often thought of writing fiction: with a step that started already in midair. It was that first, crucial step, the one that lifted you above the earth and held you there, that required a leap of faith. (What was it that student had asked me earlier—Did I think of writing as an act of faith? Maybe, I thought, I did.) Every time it seemed impossible. But after that step was built, no matter how far from the ground it floated, if it was solid, the rest of the stairs could be laid.

It seemed that Zoë's students had discovered a similar principle: that a story was a thing you could trust to take you somewhere else. And better yet, that acting as other people could allow you to say things where you were and weren't yourself.

The most interesting thing, she said, was how this dynamic played out in the classroom. Many of her students, especially at the start of a term, were deathly quiet. She had learned to be patient with them, letting the silence fill the room. Invariably the tension would build until at last someone spoke, and then more would follow, their responses ping-ponging around the desks. But in their essays and reading responses, nearly all the students—even the ones who had never spoken in class—described vivid, thriving psychological worlds full of interactions online. She felt she knew her students in a strange, doubled sense: the selves that sat in her classroom, eyes dropped to their notebooks, and the selves that they wrote about, the ones that performed and cavorted on the internet. It was as though—and she did recognize this tendency in herself—it was easier for them to express themselves in writing. As though speaking, though less permanent, would somehow be too loud to bear. Listening to her, I was reminded of what Henry had told me about his relationship with Aya: that it had started in writing, too.

In the waning days of our relationship, my ex and I tried pretending to be other people. We didn't buy outfits, or wigs, though perhaps we should have; it might have made things easier if we had drawn a clear distinction between ourselves and the roles we played. Instead, it often started as a flirtation. I'd show up at the bar late and ask, Do you come here often? He'd already be seated, a cocktail in hand. Sure, he'd say. But I haven't seen you around, have I? We'd go back and forth, enjoying the banter, but there would always be a point at which one of us would ask, So, are you waiting for someone?

I don't like pretending to sell you out, he'd say, the veil falling away. I am waiting for you.

And it was true that once the fantasy was punctured I didn't like pretending that I—the real me, the one who loved him—didn't exist.

It was best when we were both recognizably not us. That way there was no chance of hurting our own feelings. There was one fantasy we enjoyed, where we were both strangers who had come to town, encountering each other for just one night. Our roles changed whenever we played it; one of the last times, he was a musician on tour and I was the fan who had come to see him perform. Many of our charades had this tenor of power differential; he was always the one for whom its gradient was in favor, and neither of us ever questioned this. We'd meet up somewhere we'd never patronize—a restaurant on the Upper West Side; a hotel bar in Times Square—and start the evening in character. I liked seeing him through someone else's eyes, but as the night went on, our true selves, or what we thought were our true selves, would come out, and we'd end up poking fun at the people we were pretending to be. We'd become united in our mutual superiority, and the whole affair would start to feel greasy and indulgent. When we returned home, we were grateful to be us again, with all our preferences and pleasures. It made us appreciate what we had, which was each other, and the life we had designed for ourselves. But this peace would only last for so long, born as it was out of the humiliation of other, imagined people, and recalling it, I was ashamed we had ever thought it would be an antidote to our fundamental breakdown, which was that we no longer knew how to speak to each other honestly.

In the car, the radio fuzzed out, and Zoë reached for the knob to find a new station, landing on a Top 40 channel. After a few minutes, that signal faded too, and we sat in silence. In the distance, I saw a long row of white windmills turning. As we drove, it seemed there was a whole grid of them installed across the plains, more appearing with each mile.

At night, Zoë said, there's a red light on them that flashes. I think it's to prevent planes from crashing into them. What's strange is that the lights blink in unison. I don't know how they're synchronized, but all across the plains, they flash at the same time.

Every single one?

As far as I can tell.

The windmills turned and turned, and from the car their movement seemed slow, ungainly, the only elegance of it the long white arms narrowing into rounded points. Even if the lights synchronized at night, it was impossible that their turning and twirling ever would.

Is it strange, on tour? Zoë asked. Being away from home for so long?

A line of windmills scrolled by, then another. No, I said, I'm enjoying it, actually.

I was quiet for a moment, deciding how to phrase it, what to share and when. I just got out of a long relationship, I said.

We had been together for five years, I told her, and were living together when I sold my book. I hadn't told my ex that I had written a book at all, and at first he was congratulatory, if surprised and a little confused. But as the novel's publication date neared, I grew increasingly snappish and tense, and we began to pick fights with each other, nearly every day. Most of them precipitated by me. I knew I was anxious about the book—about how it, and I, would be received—and a great deal of it was drawn from events that I hadn't shared with anyone before, not even my ex. I had tried to explain this without hedging or cowardice, but I'd . . .

I turned my head to follow a streak of yellow as it rushed past the window, a field of sunflowers.

I'd kept too much from him, I said. Though I'd had to, I thought. And I think I became someone he didn't recognize, I said. And we grew miserable, and we stopped having things to say to each other, except for when we fought. When he told me he'd met someone else, it came as a relief. Like the closing of a door. Then it became easy to leave.

I'm sorry, Zoë said.

It's okay, I said.

It's a kind of a relief when a door closes, isn't it? she said. But there's also a sadness to it. I've been thinking about that lately. It seems to come up more often as I get older. All the doors I'm walking past, and which ones might close one day, and which ones I'll never open.

What do you mean by that? I asked.

I hadn't planned on getting into a serious relationship here, Zoë explained. Though maybe no one ever does, right. If you do, it never works out. That's how it always seems to go—the more you want something, it never comes, but the more you avoid it, the more that thing specifically comes to you.

She'd met a woman, she told me, at a party. Her name was Karo, a bit younger than either of us, and they clicked immediately. Within a few weeks, they were spending nearly every night together—it had been so seamless, so natural, Zoë said. By now it had been several months. They had traveled together during Zoë's spring break; they were even thinking about getting a dog. All of this was fine; it was secure, good, undramatic. Yet something had occurred recently that made her reconsider the relationship.

They had gone out to dinner at a restaurant that was connected to a brewery, about a half-hour drive away. They had been there before and that night hadn't ordered anything unusual, but near the end of the meal, Karo's face began to swell with small, puffy red hives. The outbreak worsened quickly—by the time they paid the bill and left in a hurry, one of Karo's eyes was nearly swollen shut. Zoë raced them to the hospital, where Karo was promptly treated and given a shot of steroids, as well as a set of two EpiPens to take home.

Karo never found out what had prompted such a severe reaction that night. Once the swelling went down, she had an allergy test done at the university health center. When she came out she had a grid of dots on her arm, all of them perplexingly flat. For a while, every meal Karo ate was tainted with dread. She insisted on cooking for herself, and even grocery shopping became fraught: She could buy only the brands she was used to buying; substitutions overwhelmed her. After a few weeks of this, during which Karo grew progressively more anxious, they realized they couldn't continue living that way, and they went out to restaurants again. Karo kept both EpiPens in her bag.

It's made me think about how much we don't know about ourselves until we're forced to learn, Zoë said. Karo didn't know what she was allergic to. She still doesn't know. It could be anything, you know? And it's frightened her. Even though she's going out in the world again, I can tell she wants to keep her life small.

She couldn't tell, either, how much of this smallness was new, and how much of it was a smallness that she had either inadvertently or willingly ignored. It was true that after the incident, Karo refused to try nearly any new restaurant or type of food. But even before it, had she been just as cautious about new experiences? Zoë couldn't remember. They didn't like the same types of films or television. They hadn't yet spoken about children. They both loved the outdoors, Zoë said. And living together was easy, she added, and pleasant. I think— she began, then stopped. I think, if she could, Karo would want to continue like this, here, forever.

We drove past a field where some horses were standing around. Two were close together; one was on its own. Another was grazing, its head low to the ground. They passed by so quickly I craned my neck to look but couldn't make out their colors.

It's easy to find ourselves sliding into situations, I said.

We made choices every day, I thought, and the accumulation of those choices could feel like nothing, because there was so much that seemed out of our control. Then, suddenly, we were met with the consequences of our actions, so layered and inevitable that it felt like we didn't choose them at all.

Aloud I said: I guess I would ask you if that's really what you want, or what you think you want, and also, are you coming up with excuses for why you do or don't want something.

I'm worried that—no, actually, I'm not worried, Zoë said, and I knew that she wasn't, and that *worried* wasn't the word she meant.

I'm considering that if I break up with her now, she'll take it as a betrayal, she said. That she'll think it's because of what happened that night. And it'll feel like I'm abandoning her in her time of need.

But it's not about that, I said.

It's not about that, she agreed.

We passed another field of windmills, each the tallest thing around, so tall they didn't beget any comparison. I couldn't picture how big a house was, or a tree; I couldn't picture anything but the windmills' white, alien shapes, turning and turning.

It's starting to affect my sleep, Zoë said. Thinking about whether to stay or to go. She changed her posture suddenly, sitting up straight and arching her back.

Do I go through? she said aloud, not looking at me, as if talking only to herself. Will it change me?

Her profile was a clean shape against the soybean fields.

Maybe, I said, you and Karo can get into role-play, and for the first time, she laughed.

What my ex and I had never learned was how the act of being someone else can set the true self free. When we pretended, we layered on levels of artifice. Instead of revealing something we couldn't say any other way, we just covered everything up.

We arrived in the late afternoon. As I was getting out of the car, my phone lit up with an email notification. I glanced at the screen.

One line, no subject.

That's not how I remember it.

He'd found me, then.

Hey, Zoë said. I was standing outside the car, the passenger door still open. She had taken my suitcase out of the trunk and was waiting for me.

Hey, are you okay?

I closed my eyes and, after a brief effort, opened them again.

I'm fine, I said.

———

After college, I had gone straight into an MFA program for painting. A professor I'd worked with in undergrad had just left to direct the graduate program at a different university. In his class—advanced painting studio, spring of my junior year—I had started to make the work that would eventually become my thesis. The next fall, after he had arrived at the new program, he invited me to apply.

At the time, I was making what I called *studies*, small paintings that I completed in a single sitting. After two years of introductory art classes, arranged around the development of technical skills and by-the-book assignments that didn't play to my strengths, it had taken me some time to find my style, which was fast, fluid, and unforced, focused almost entirely on gesture. The content of what I painted nearly didn't matter—I made paintings of interiors, self-portraits, portraits of friends and acquaintances—only that I worked from life, which itself was a vehicle for that gesture. It was as though there was something in each subject I wanted to capture, some quirk of its or their aliveness, and if I worked quickly enough, channeling the paint through a nearly oracular means, I was able to arrive at a place where others could see what I had seen. I used the same palette for all my paintings, and often just one brush, letting the colors blend together. My canvases were still wet during critique.

I had trouble talking about my work, for it so often seemed to arrive without language—was pre-language, in fact—and what unified it wasn't subject matter but the physicality of how it was made. Yet when the work was going well I was wildly prolific; when I was stalled, I might be stalled for weeks. My process involved sitting on the floor of my studio for hours at a time, until something called to me—what was it?—and I leaped. I was as obedient to that call as a dog.

Though I hadn't planned to go to graduate school, I was encour-

aged by the professor's interest in my work, and I applied. The program was new, only a year or two old, and I thought that, plus the
recommendation from him, was the reason I got in. It was a surprise
to me when I won a departmental award that spring, one traditionally
presented to a female art major in the graduating class. The validation
it provided made me feel like I really was an artist, that this immersion
in art was not just a brief period before my adult life began but could
in fact be my real life, my whole life, and using the prize money to pay
my deposit, I enrolled in the MFA that fall.

When I arrived at the program, in a midsize city not far from
where I had done undergrad but where I knew no one and had no
friends, I found I had trouble continuing the momentum that had carried me through the end of college. The city felt unfriendly. I had
trouble sleeping. My work was supposed to develop and mature beyond what I had already made, but I didn't have a clear sense of how
to move forward. During my first week in the program, I did nothing
but pace over my empty canvases, gessoing and re-gessoing their surfaces until they were as smooth and blank as ice. All my usual subjects
were gone—my friends, my familiar interiors—and with no one else
to paint, the professor encouraged me to focus on self-portraiture. I
did as he instructed, making paintings of my body and my face. At
first he praised me for it, and in time, I learned the reason he had instructed me to apply, which was that he wanted me in a different place,
close to him, where he could proceed to isolate me.

That wasn't how it felt then; maybe that's only how I was able to
phrase it years later, with the distance of time and the ability to nar-
rativize both myself and the event. How it felt then was that I had
been discovered as an artist, and that my particular way of seeing was
luminous, valuable, perhaps even genius. How it felt at the time was
that he invited me to dinner at the house he was allotted from the col-

lege, a stately Victorian with warm yellow light in every room. How it felt was that I had no one in my life to tell, not anymore: Many of my classmates had moved to other parts of the country, and I had fallen out with my closest friend from college.

Without my realizing it, my life had become small; he was the one thing that promised to make it larger.

It began that fall. The dinners, the drinks, the encouragement during critique, the studio visits that lingered into the evening. Perhaps it would have all turned out fine if it stayed that way. If it had been merely a little too friendly, a little too cozy, which was, I was learning then, how most connections in the culture industry were formed and maintained. There was an aura about the professor in those days, an aura of power, and charisma, and wildness. He'd only been at the program for a year but had already become known for the gatherings—lush, sophisticated—that he held. A classmate of mine had even expressed envy that I had worked with him in undergrad and that he was already familiar with my practice. You're so lucky he already likes you, the classmate said.

He likes me, I remembered thinking. Was that what it was?

I was liked; I was special. I was twenty-two and told I was a budding star. And I wanted it. It was exciting to know the professor, exciting to talk to him and feel the ferociousness of his full attention, exciting when he banged open the studio door in the night to see who was still working, and I was proud that I always was. I liked how it felt to be watched, to be perceived as the pure artist I hoped I was becoming. He was the sort of person everyone turned to when he entered a room; you knew where he was at every party. Or maybe—I wondered this now—I had just learned to look for him. As the weeks went by and the air cooled, we grew close.

In December, I spent winter break on campus instead of going home to see my parents, who hadn't approved of my decision to go to graduate school. The professor knew I would be alone for the holiday; I told him most everything, and he listened. Three days before Christmas, he invited me to spend the weekend with him in the mountains, in a region where many artists had historically lived and worked. Why don't we take a field trip, was what he said. There was art he could show me. People he wanted to introduce me to.

I knew, even then, that his asking me placed our relationship on a precipice. There had always been danger and excitement in our relations, which made me feel fizzy and giddy at best and desperately anxious at worst. But I knew it was more than a matter of wanting or not wanting to go. I wanted to stay in his good graces. I wanted to learn from him, to meet the people he wanted me to meet. I wanted to trust him. I wanted him to be what he said he was, which was my mentor, and friend.

If I had had someone to talk to. If I had been a little wiser, or a little less lonely, maybe I could have known to give him just enough, never too much; that would have made me the one in control. But I wasn't, and perhaps the possibility of ever having been in control was a fantasy I granted myself only in retrospect.

Take the train to P———, he said. I'll come meet you.

By the time I arrived, the decision seemed inevitable. The relationship, already so charged, had changed and flared into different colors, pushed along by a current that felt larger than I was.

Up the narrow stairs. The sconced lights. The white room with its made bed.

I would do this, and I would do that, and I thought I wouldn't do that, though I did.

———

I thought, now, of Zoë's closing doors, the rooms of her life that she feared were forever to be undisturbed. The choices she had made; the choices we all make. Had I been the one closing mine as we walked down that hallway, or was it he who closed them for me, reaching across my form? And which of us was it who went first through that final door?

When I returned to campus, I tried to paint again, but I couldn't stop my hands from shaking. In the hallways of the art building, which was large and gray and labyrinthine, seeing the professor rattled me. Before the trip, I'd understood our relationship to exist within the safe confines of the university. Now that boundary had collapsed. I could only see that other, starkly different version of him—that distinguished old painter, cresting toward the peak of his career, whom everyone had treated with such deference on our trip. He had withdrawn from me after we returned from the mountains. I waited for him to invite me again to dinner, and after a week of his silence wondered what exactly I was waiting for. He no longer stepped into our studio in the evenings, throwing the doors open, announcing his presence. He was absent from the spring term's opening reception. I suspected he was avoiding me. I sat on the floor and painted alone.

Late that January I was assigned to one of the first critiques of the semester. I wasn't ready. My work, which had felt so revived, so luscious and full of life the previous term, haloed by the aura of dinners and drinks and praise from the old painter, had grown stale. I had forced myself to finish what was due, but I could not bear to paint myself any longer, and in the critique I showed a series of paintings that weren't good at all, my technique gone flat, the subject constantly hidden or turning away. I had hit a wall in my practice, it was clear, or was it that I was distracted by the swirl of what had happened, unable to focus on my work, either way it was lacking, and the other instructors called that out, the laziness of the painting, the lack of direction, and was I really ready, they asked, for the commitment that this program required?

If it had not been my own critique I would have called it a bloodbath. As it was, I had no choice but to take it in, nodding, my mind empty of a single thought. Through it all, I watched as the old painter sat in his chair, not disagreeing, not saying anything, tacitly siding with his colleagues, the power firmly banked on his side. And—even now I was still ashamed of this, of having done this—I looked to him, my eyes calling to him, willing him to defend me, to say a word of praise, to reassure them of my potential. I had wanted him to save me.

But he didn't look at me, he never looked at me, and after the crit, as I was packing up my things, I heard two of my classmates talking in low voices outside the room. They were speaking of my era as the favorite and how it had come to an ignominious end. I hadn't realized that it had been so obvious—had it been that obvious?—and I had not realized that there were rewards I could have pursued, rewards I had not claimed.

I was young then, but I was old enough to be humiliated; old enough to feel ashamed for letting it happen—and I could not articulate properly what had happened—and I felt responsible, somehow, for allowing the change to take place. If only things could have continued as they were. If only he had not asked me to come. If only—

After the critique, I started avoiding the studio, working only in the very early morning hours, before anyone else was awake. Rather than being motivated to work harder out of spite or revenge, I lost all faith in painting. The oil colors on my palette scabbed over and dried. I didn't finish any new work.

Eventually I took a leave of absence without finishing out the year and, after a protracted bureaucratic battle, formally withdrew from

the program. I moved to New York, where I got an entry-level job in
arts administration and began to pay off my student loans. As far as I
knew, the old painter was still teaching. In fact, not long after I left the
program, before the school removed me from its mailing list, I learned
he had been made dean. He was just famous enough that sometimes I
encountered his name, or his work, in places that I didn't expect, and
it always jolted me. A month before I left for my tour he'd had a retrospective in the city that received middling reviews, but I couldn't
escape the press for it, or the postcards, which seemed to be everywhere, printed with a color image of one of his paintings, violet and
gray and green.

I had never been able to take myself seriously as an artist after everything that happened, even though in the larger timeline of my life it
had been only a few months. I didn't paint again. It was too hard to
decouple my work from my body, which felt like something I was carrying around, burdened with and stained by association.

When I started writing and began to publish essays and criticism,
I didn't use an author photo. I wrote under my first and middle ini-
tials, obscuring my full name. My tone as a critic was diligent, well
read, faintly old-fashioned; I never wrote about my own life. When,
after a few years, I began to publish fiction, my stories were short,
oblique, and ran in undersubscribed, print-only magazines. On social
media, where I mainly lurked, my avatar was a picture of a small,
fuzzy plastic figurine of a baby bear wearing a yellow raincoat. I enjoyed the anonymity that all of this provided me, how my life as a
writer had begun as a perfectly blank slate.

But with the publication of my novel—a book I had chosen to
write and the publication of which I had sought—my life as an anon-

ymous writer changed. Suddenly I was a writer, and not any writer but a woman writer. Even during editorial meetings, I had begun to notice that people responded to me a certain way after meeting me in person, once they knew how I looked and dressed, and that that, coupled with the content of my book, made them treat me with a kind of intrigue that sometimes bordered on the sexual. It was as though, having met me, and knowing what they thought they knew about me, vis-à-vis my book, they expected me to be a specific kind of person, a specific kind of woman, and were delighted when I behaved in a way that met their expectations.

I was deeply suspicious of the pleasure I derived from these interactions, but I did take pleasure in them. In seeing people turn and smile when I entered a room. The hands, reaching out to welcome me in.

And within these pleasures lived a familiar tension, one I had first encountered when I was young. When my work had been inseparable from the body that made it, the body that stretched canvases and poured gesso and moved with brush in hand. It was the pain of not being certain whether I was being praised for my talent—my mind, which felt more and more like the only thing that was my own—or because I looked and acted a certain way, a way that fit a narrative. There was much to desire about being desired; I had learned that, same as anyone. When I was a student, I had thought I could manipulate that gaze to a certain extent, that I had agency. That being desired gave me power. But what I learned then, and what I understood now, was that though one might thrust an oar into the river and think herself steering her own way, the current pushes on, uncaring.

There was a time when I was traveling very often for work. I had landed a plum assignment, a write-up of a new art fair in Shanghai and the burgeoning contemporary-art scene there. This was some years ago, when flying felt cheap and easy and inconsequential; I had quit my job to write full-time. Nothing much happened during the trip itself, but on my flight back to the States I was stopped during security because a lighter, which I had accidentally smuggled into the country, showed up on the X-ray of my carry-on. Meanwhile, the Australian businessman behind me in line had struck up a conversation, which at first I entertained. He wanted to know where I was coming from, and why I was in China, and if I was Chinese, which I wasn't, and at first I answered politely while I removed my electronics from my pockets and placed them in the screening bins. But after I was stopped my responses grew more curt, and he continued to stand over me, blithely packing his own possessions, watching and talking as I unzipped every compartment of my suitcase and dug through my folded clothes to find the offending lighter, which was in the pocket of a pair of pants I hadn't even worn. I was dressed in a ratty long-sleeved shirt and leggings that sagged in the rear; my hair was unwashed and unbrushed; I grew sweaty, my face reddening, as I shoved my things back into my suitcase, and after what felt like far too long, he eventually went on his way to his flight. He had been hitting on me, I understood, but what I didn't understand was why he had done it. I was a complete stranger to him. We weren't on the same flight, were going to completely different parts of the terminal. I was not going to sleep with him; I was not going to give him my phone number; I had nothing in the way of professional connections to offer. What had he been trying to obtain?

It occurred to me now that the absence of any meaning was the point. I wasn't the subject of the interaction; I had been no one to him.

Packing for my book tour, I had chosen my clothes carefully. I knew I was going to be away from home for a while, in a variety of situations and climates. Early in my life I had come to believe in clothing and fashion as armor, and it was that armor that I drew on now as I dressed in my room at the college, a guest room in a house where visiting speakers and members of the board often stayed. Before my trip I had been tempted to buy a whole new wardrobe, in keeping with the upheaval in the rest of my life; I had even wanted to cut my hair, to become yet again another person. I still could, I thought. There was always time to become another version of one's self. But then I was brushing my hair back from my face, and smoothing the fabric of the dress that had wrinkled in transit, and then I couldn't think about any of it anymore because it was nearly six and I was due at dinner.

I looked at my phone, opened my email, read the message again, closed it, locked the screen, and left it in my room.

After the dinner, I walked down the main street to a bar that Zoë had recommended as a good option for a nightcap. It's a townie bar, she had said approvingly; you won't run into anyone there. Not, I thought, that I knew anyone from anyone else.

A black-and-white cat padded in front of me as I entered the bar, weaving between my legs; it disappeared into a corner. There was a long counter, with vinyl stools, and two pool tables in the back. A jukebox was installed next to a table, three young men crowded around its glowing screen. Next to the jukebox hung a framed print of an Edward Hopper painting of a woman wearing a hat, drinking coffee alone; streaks and smudges marked the glass. A squat jar of pickled eggs, white and floating in brine, sat on the counter, next to a jar of maraschino cherries. Everything seemed lit from below, the red of the cherries vibrating in the blue lights. I took a seat at the bar and ordered a whiskey soda.

She always does this, one of the young men said now, with feeling.

I looked up. He was tall, with floppy hair, and wore a hooded sweat-shirt. He held up his phone to show his friends, but from where I sat I couldn't see the screen. In his other hand he held a vape pen.

She likes you, his friend said.

The three young men were talking, unselfconsciously and in loud voices, about a scenario I didn't understand. It seemed that one of them, the tall one, who was also the most handsome of the group, had begun seeing a girl who lived in a nearby town. From his reports, the relationship was going well, although he declined to describe it as dating. We're talking, he said. They had met through their social circle, and she had independent friendships with some of his other friends, including one of the men who was sitting at the table, scrolling through songs on the jukebox. What was confusing, the tall one said, was that sometimes she would send him pictures of herself from his friends' phones. He'd open his messages from Tyler, for instance—that must have been his friend at the jukebox—and see her grinning face, one hand making a peace sign. Sometimes she even sent him quasi-romantic messages, which disconcerted him when they appeared on his phone, arriving not under her name but under the names of his friends.

She likes you, Tyler repeated amiably, not looking up from the jukebox screen.

She wants you to know she's thinking about you, said their other friend, who was broad-shouldered and had a large beard. Even when she's hanging out with other people.

But why can't she just tell me using her own name?

Maybe she's shy, the bearded friend offered.

Tyler selected a song on the jukebox, and music began to play.

Stop letting her take your phone, the tall one said.

Tyler shrugged. Not hurting anyone, he said.

A car drove by, its headlights refracting into the bar, gleaming off the framed Hopper print, briefly illuminating the woman's face. I finished my drink, though I had been trying to go slowly, and ordered another. I finished that drink, too, and ordered a third. The colored lights in the bar and the sound of the music and the overheard conversation all mingled together to take me slightly out of my body, so that I felt as though I had never been myself before and would never be myself again.

I was not thinking about the email I had received. No. I was thinking about Josephine Hopper, who had modeled for her husband's paintings. I had never liked the way Hopper painted women, how he reduced them to broody, buxom figures with indistinct features. All his women had the same face, in fact, round and snub-nosed with a pointed chin. In a high school art class someone told me Jo had been tyrannically jealous of her husband's practice, and that was why she insisted he use no other model. In his paintings she is young, old, blond, or redheaded; she is a secretary, a dancer, a woman waiting for an order of chop suey. But it's always her.

It wasn't until years later that I read about Josephine's own career and learned that she had been a painter herself, a protégée of Robert Henri's. There is a portrait of her, too, painted by Henri. Only her face and hands are in bright light, the rest dropped away into shadow. Her face is vivid; her pursed lips give her an expression of intense focus. For years she had been the more famous artist; when she met Edward, she helped him get into a show at the Brooklyn Museum, launching his career. After, her own was eclipsed. Yet she took an active role in his work; she acquired costumes, created characters, participated wholeheartedly in the fantasy. She referred to his paintings as their children. They fought bitterly and often, but it's Josephine who appears beside Edward in his final painting, two clowns at the edge of a stage, taking their last bow.

What was the world they had built together—that imagined, lonely place where neither of them was happy, but both could speak?

I looked at the print on the wall, but the woman's face held no answers. She looked like she was in a hurry: one hand gloved, the other bare.

Can I buy you a drink? said a voice. It was Tyler, who had broken from his friends to stand next to me at the bar.

Sure, I said.

I'm Tyler, he said, though I already knew that. I had been listening to them talk for nearly an hour now.

I'm Christine, I said.

At dinner, the department chair had spoken to me as though he already knew who I was and what I liked. Eventually I realized it was because he had read my novel and assumed it to be autobiographical. Though he wasn't wrong, I had wanted to be contrary. None of that happened, I had wanted to say, but didn't. Instead I had listened, with a small, alert smile on my face, as he explained my own book to me, and what he thought it was about.

You're not from here, are you? Tyler said. The bartender passed me a glass, wordlessly. When I picked it up, it left a wet ring on the counter.

I'm just passing through, I said.

What brings you here?

I took a sip of my new drink. It was late enough in the evening that it no longer tasted like anything, though I didn't feel drunk.

Work, I said.

When I left the MFA program, snow was still on the ground. Crocuses were beginning to appear in the mulch around city-planted trees. I had made a post on a local platform to give away my art supplies, and a young woman came to pick them up. She wasn't affiliated with the school—burning with shame, I hadn't wanted to tell my cohort that I was emptying my studio—and, after looking over the items I had laid out, she took everything. The stretcher bars, the canvas roll, the oil paints and cloudy jars of mineral spirits, each with its metal coil in the bottom; the brushes and scrapers and palette knives; the tub of gesso, the sanding sponge, the roller and the housepainter's brush—all of it went into her giant vinyl shopping bag. She even took the glass palette, still caked with dried oil paint. When I apologized for its condition, she told me that she would use a razor blade to scrape it clean. I kind of like it, she said. The scraping.

After, I sat on the floor of my empty studio. I felt a dull, cold sadness that turned into a numbness, and after the numbness had spread to my entire body, I stood and left the room.

Later, I understood that what I felt was the feeling of having given up on a dream. I wished that I had kept something from that studio, something from that time in my life. A sketchbook; a gum eraser. But I had discarded everything.

Tyler put one elbow on the bar and leaned closer to me, as though he wanted to more clearly hear what I was saying. What do you do for work, then?

I'm a figure skater, I said.

Here, in this bar, where no one knew me and I knew no one, I wanted to be someone else. To play a role I had never before played. I knew that there was no ice rink in this town, but that didn't matter. I delivered the lie like it was true, and in saying it, I became it.

His friends saw us talking and turned to face us.

A figure skater in Grinnell, he said. I looked at the expressionless face of the woman in the Hopper print. *Automat*, I remembered. That was the name of the painting.

Why not? I said.

He looked at me, closely, and I held his gaze, not moving my eyes or my mouth.

And I imagined myself as I knew they must be imagining me then, a woman in a glittering dress, arms outstretched, carving paths onto the dark ice.

Is she busy? No. But she's working. The artist stands before her canvas with her hands on her hips. Two triangles of negative space in the air. He wants to thrust a hand through each one.

Then can he take a look? Fine. Sure. She steps aside. He looks for a long time. Here, he says. Here, what does he mean *here*? There. He points. She looks for what he is seeing. There. She can feel the heat of his attention. It concentrates to a point at the start of her spine. The surface of her body comes alight. That's what painting is, surfaces. She says this aloud. She hears him agree.

When he finally leaves her studio she finds that her skin is sheened all over with a thin layer of sweat.

FRANKENTHALER

wake and I feel no pain, Colin said. The server came by to refill our water. I was drinking an old-fashioned, very slowly, and a sparkling coat of perspiration beaded my glass. In the warm late-afternoon light, the orange peel glowed in the bottom of my drink, shifting every time I took a sip.

I sleep well, for eight hours each night, and every morning I feel confident in the decisions I made the night before. I go to work, complete all my tasks, and have time to do the things that bring me happiness. I cook, I clean, and I enjoy taking the time to make my home comfortable. I have no regrets about the choices I've made, and I can remember everything perfectly, including my dreams.

He sat in front of me, his posture loose, legs spread wide, hands lightly resting on his knees. We were seated outside a restaurant that hadn't existed the last time I visited my hometown, the city where he now lived. It had been his suggestion. When we met for dinner he had informed me that he was sober and I told him I was proud of him. I'll be fine if you drink, he assured me. I knew he was telling the truth.

We had dated during my early years in New York, where our relationship had centered on drinking and going out. Through that drinking, a void opened up for him that never opened for me, and it had turned out to be a place that I couldn't go with him. Nor could I be the one to lead him away. The relationship ended after he left the city for graduate school, which had been—nearly eight years ago, we concluded. He hadn't finished his degree, but instead dropped out and taught himself how to code, and now he worked at a tech company that had moved its headquarters to the Pacific Northwest not long ago. When he saw I would be in town for a book event, he reached out and suggested we have dinner. I could tell, even with his clothes on, that he had been working out, and he looked healthy.

It happened when I went on a backpacking trip, Colin said. This was when I was still at MIT. It was the start of my fourth year in the program. Late September. The weather was cooling, and I felt I had made a good start on my research, and I wanted to hike the Midstate Trail for a few days. I had planned to go alone. I usually traveled alone—I still do, he added, glancing at me. It's good to be alone, he said. I told my adviser I'd be offline and packed a bag. I was planning to be away for four days.

I had been drinking before the trip, he said. I didn't consider it a lot, but it was. I could finish a fifth of whiskey in a day. No matter what I was doing, I always had a glass of something with me. Like an IV drip. I had been drinking like that for months. When I left, I packed a bottle with me, but it was heavy, and I didn't want to carry much.

The first night, it was fine. I set up my tent and got out my stove and made some food out of a packet. I drank about a third of the bottle. I was pleased, because drinking made my pack lighter. The second night, I thought I would be fine. I set up camp again, but that evening I drank more, more than I had planned for. I began to get nervous when I realized I hadn't brought enough. My hands started shaking uncontrollably, and I couldn't sleep. My mind was racing, trying to figure out where exactly on the trail I was, and if there was a town nearby where I could hike out to get more. But I was too far out and didn't have cell service, and eventually, when the sun came up, I started hiking again. I was so tired it was all I could do to put one foot in front of the other. It was a wooded section, and there was no getting off trail, not for another twenty miles. That evening I set up camp by a lake. The sky was clear, and the moon was out. I finished what I had brought and it helped for a moment, but not for long enough, and the anxiety immediately came back. I didn't have the energy to cook, but I was too sick to sleep. All I could do was sit in front of my tent and stare at the water. As the night darkened, I could see the stars with more and more clarity. There were so many patterns and shapes I could draw between them that I felt overwhelmed, and I had to stop trying to focus on individual stars. Then it grew so dark I could even see the Milky Way. I hadn't seen it in years. All of it—the stars, the Milky Way, the moon—was reflected in the lake. It was one of the most beautiful things I'd ever seen. And I was sweating, and my hands were shaking, and all I could think about was how badly I wanted a drink.

The next morning I got off trail and bought two tallboys of malt liquor at a gas station, he said. I drank one and I felt better, and then I felt sick, and I started crying. I opened the second one, but before I could drink it, I threw up in the parking lot. I called Nick—do you remember Nick?—and he drove from Providence to get me. I was a mess. I was covered in puke, my shoes were covered in it, my bag was covered in it, and he put me in the back seat. He drove me back to Boston. I was cradling the can in my hands, drinking from it like a baby. I didn't even want to drink at that point, but I had to or I'd be sick. The whole drive, we had just one exchange. I said to him, Nick, I have to stop this. And he said yes, you do.

Colin closed his eyes. I took a sip of my water and he opened them again. I could tell from the way that his arm shook slightly that he was bouncing his leg under the table, though we weren't touching.

I remembered how, when we had dated, I would lose track of him at parties, and find him hunched over in the bathroom, his eyes red-rimmed and watery. I would refuse to kiss him then, his mouth sour and awful, but the nights where he threw up and had to be taken home were better than the ones where he blacked out, and was loud, and made belligerent conversation, his eyes staring straight ahead, seeing nothing.

Sex, when it happened between us, had been either fantastic or terrible. Most of the time it didn't happen at all. We'd get home in a blur and I'd wake, brutally hungover and mostly clothed, in his apartment, half the sheets pulled off the mattress, my legs tangled up in a blanket, while he slept next to me, his brow unmarked, jaw slack. But there were times when we first met, before it got bad and difficult, before he went to that place where I couldn't follow, when we arrived at parties together, gleaming like main characters, and charmed everyone around us, and went home at the right time or even sooner. It was that Colin I missed when I began to miss him while we were still dating, the adventurous one, who climbed up fire escapes and onto roofs, who had an edge to him, an edge he tested against me, but I didn't mind. Sitting across from him, I could remember the hardness of his body, how thin his skin seemed in contrast to the swell of his muscles, the greenish veins branched out underneath. His sweat then had smelled of whiskey; when we slept together, I imagined it seeping into the mattress beneath our bodies, like a stain. I never thought about how I smelled when I was with him. But I must have smelled the same way.

What did you do after that? I asked him.

I finished out the semester, he said. Barely. What was strange, he said, was that no one seemed to notice the shift that had occurred in me. That Wednesday, I showed up for my weekly meeting with my adviser on time, and she didn't even ask about my trip. None of the faculty noticed. None of my cohort noticed. But everything about me was different. The way I moved through the world had changed, and I could never go back. Maybe, he said, leaning forward, as though it had just occurred to him, maybe it was a sign of how isolated I had become. That no one except for Nick knew what I was going through. At the end of the term, I left.

Did you ever join AA? I asked.

He shook his head. No, he said. I probably should have. I wanted to do it on my own. I was stubborn that way.

I know that, I said, and he smiled a little.

They ask you to believe in a higher power over there, he said. But I couldn't bring myself to believe in one, and when I tried to rationalize it, I kept coming to the same conclusion: that if a higher power existed, it wouldn't have allowed me to get to that place.

You don't believe in a god who loves you, I said.

No, he said, I don't.

The waiter came by again and though I had finished my drink, I didn't order another. I asked for a seltzer and it came in a slim blue bottle, next to an equally slender glass. I could feel Colin watching me as I twisted open the cap and poured. The carbonation fizzed up, freckling the back of my hand, and I wiped it on a napkin.

Are you excited about the book? he asked me.

I'm not sure, I said. Yes. Maybe.

He didn't know why I had left graduate school, and in my desire to reinvent myself in New York, I never told him. I had hoped my status as a dropout gave me an aura of mystery, but the truth was that I hadn't been doing much of anything when we met. I was working in arts administration at the job I had immediately taken when I moved, and at the time, I hadn't written a word, or even begun to conceive of myself as someone who could be a writer. Instead, I dreaded watching the sun set, the way it drew each day to such a damning close, reminding me of all the things I hadn't accomplished, and when it turned out that Colin and I worked in the same area, a quickly gentrifying industrial neighborhood by the water, it became easy to sit together in a dive bar at the end of each workday, hiding from that terrible sunset, until it was fully dark out and we could walk to the train beneath the small, personable glow of the sodium streetlights. It was on one of those evenings he had first kissed me, cupping the back of my head in his big hand, fingers splayed in my hair, loosening the knot I wore it in then.

The sun was setting now. My phone, which had been resting on the table, buzzed with a call, but it wasn't a number I recognized, and I silenced it. Lately I had been getting calls from area codes I'd never lived in, but I assumed they were the automated scam calls everyone was getting. Whenever I picked up, no one answered, and once, the number that had shown up on the caller ID was mine. Colin raised his eyebrows.

It's just a spam call, I said. I put my phone back in my bag and told him about the book and the tour that I had planned for myself.

I had started writing in earnest while we were still dating. My job involved supporting artists and writers, and though my role wasn't editorial, because our staff was small, I was often asked to edit submissions and blog posts. The organization's blog wasn't particularly widely read, yet I admired how a rough draft could transform into a polished work, a text that could be shared and circulated. I saw the process again and again, that something out of nothing—how writing made palpable the intangibility of a thought. Eventually I worked up the courage to write my own post. Then I wrote another. Then I wrote more, for other outlets.

It wasn't until after Colin left for his PhD program and we broke up that I considered the possibility of writing full-time. When I eventually left my job, I wrote him an email, telling him about the decision, though we hadn't really been talking. It had felt important to let him know, because he had seen and known me when I was just starting out.

The novel, however, I had started thinking about two years later, during a season in which it seemed like every woman on the internet was coming forward with a story of sexist mistreatment at the hands of a wealthy and powerful man. It was these women's stories, plain-spoken, unembellished, and delivered at terrible personal risk, that allowed me to write my own book, I understood.

But Colin didn't know that, and I wasn't certain that I wanted to tell him, not here, not in this way. Aloud I said, And now I have the great good fortune—it was supposed to be good fortune, wasn't it?—of getting to travel and talk about it.

That's wonderful, he said. You always wanted to travel, didn't you?

I was surprised that he remembered, but he was right, I had.

He wanted to know my route and I told him, and he nodded approvingly at the stops I had chosen, and the time I had allotted at each. That's a good itinerary, he said, I wouldn't have planned it differently. You're not going to see your family while you're here?

No, I said, I don't think so. I hadn't ever really talked about my family with him before and I didn't want to start now. I looked at the bubbles collecting on the inside of my glass, and wanting to gracefully change the topic somehow, I reached to pick it up and instead knocked it over, the smooth side of the glass bumping against my thumb and forefinger. Sparkling water rushed through the metal grille of the outdoor table and spattered against the silk skirt I was wearing.

Oh, fuck, I said. I'm such a klutz.

You're not, he said.

I dabbed ineffectually at my skirt, which had been dove gray but was now runneled with dark streaks.

It'll dry, he said, and briefly, I hated him.

It's fine. I folded the damp napkin and set it back on the table. I think talking about my family made me nervous, I said.

The server came by again with a bar mop for me. I wadded it into a ball and placed it in my lap, feeling like an idiot.

Is that an invitation to ask about it, he said, and suddenly it was as though I were sitting with two of him: the Colin who was really in front of me, and the version of him that I had known before. I couldn't shake the dissonance I felt in front of this calm, stable man, who spoke in declarative sentences. I had never before seen him like this, which made sense, because this version of him had never existed when we knew each other.

And yet I didn't know what to do. All the memories we shared were ruinous. Tales of ways we'd hurt ourselves or each other, acted out in front of strangers. As much as I loved to dwell in memory itself, I was suspicious of nostalgia. It was too good at holding you in that moment, staining everything, like an oil, or a color. It seemed that I had two options: to slip into reminiscing with Colin, and reanimate the old vampire of his twenty-three-year-old self, not to mention mine, or else, in this tiny window of time we had chosen to reconnect, find a new mode of relating to him.

I wasn't even sure I liked this iteration of him, the one who had learned how to package his previous suffering into neat narrative. I felt guilty for missing the person he had been when he was in a bad way. It wasn't, I thought, that badness made you interesting, or that pain was what proved us to be human. I wasn't upset he was doing well. But he had lost the edges of his personality, the oppositions, the nooks and crannies I used to be able to dig a finger into and tug at to pull him closer to me. Or—I considered this—perhaps he still had those edges, but they were different now, and I had lost my referents, and could see only the pristine, immaculate self he had been smoothing and shaping for years, as if trimming pottery on a wheel. There was a stage that clay got to, I knew, before it was fired in the kiln, where it had lost some of its moisture and arrived at something called leather hardness. It was still a little flexible then, dark in color, not brittle or powdery, and it could be trimmed with a sharp tool. The walls could be thinned, the curvature of an undulating knob or the lip of a jar more clearly defined.

I wanted to push him, to test whether this new self had really become this hardened, and I kept looking for any scent of that wickedness in him I had loved. The old Colin would have never asked me about my family, not in that way. He would have breezed right past the subject, or else pinned me there and asked directly, wanting to watch me squirm.

No, I don't want to talk about it, I said.

We can talk about something else, then.

I couldn't remember what we had talked about when we were together. What conversations had we shared; what had we had to say to each other? Had we talked about books, or music, or movies? I couldn't remember seeing a single film with him.

I'm trying to remember what we talked about when we dated, I said.

We didn't talk about much, he said. Are you dating now?

No, actually, I said.

Would you like to come over?

Colin lived in the northwest quadrant of the city, where a stand of high-rise apartment buildings had sprung up in the last five years, close to the water. His apartment was nice enough that I made a noise of surprise when we walked in.

It turns out, he said, the quality of your life improves once you start making a lot of money.

Ha, I said.

The apartment had all the mid-century modern signifiers of upward mobility. A long, low couch in the living room, a record player, a swaying lamp that dimmed at a touch. When I glanced into the bedroom I saw the sheets were neatly made on his bed, which rested on a sturdy wooden frame. When we first met, he slept on a mattress on the floor, the short end pushed up against the wall.

Sit down, he said, do you want anything?

I'm fine, I said. He got me a glass of water anyway, and then he did something with the sound system I couldn't parse. Ambient electronic music began to play, just loud enough to be audible, and I had the feeling that this was something he did often, and that he had worked out a system for it, a series of touches and taps that drew up a

ritualistic barrier between his nakedly sober self and the casual sex he
was about to engage in. But I was familiar to him, I thought, and I
took some pride in that, and wondered if, with me, it would be different.

He sat on the carpet in front of me and took hold of my right shoe.
I was wearing a pair of white leather sneakers I liked to travel in. He
undid the laces and slid it off my foot, then unrolled the sock I was
wearing and placed it in the empty bowl of the shoe. He held my ankle
in his two hands, considering it, one palm wrapped around the base of
my heel, and then he kissed me, right at the hill of bone above which
there was a small tattoo of a dragonfly, the only tattoo I had. His
mouth was warm.

I forgot about this, he said.

I forget about it most of the time, I said.

He nosed along the top of my foot, following the tendons in it, his
fingers pressed flat against the arch. When I curled my toes he made a
noise of deep satisfaction, and then he kissed the inside of my knee,
pushing my skirt out of the way. The seltzer had dried, and left a faint
stain, one that would come out the next time I washed it.

He sat up, then. There was color high in his cheeks. It was almost
unbearable to look directly at him, but that hardness, that glimmering
edge that I had known before, was visible now, and I understood that
this was what it took, that it was our nakedness that would make us
most familiar to each other.

In his room, we undressed slowly. Nothing about it felt rushed. I
couldn't imagine having sex with him for the first time. I felt as though
I had always lived in the state of once having slept with him, of knowing him that way, and of him knowing me. Was that nostalgia? All the
details of his body I had forgotten were still there, and his manner-
isms. His way of frowning slightly as he entered me; the vein that

jumped above his right hip. When I put my fingers on it, I could feel his pulse. His veins were still visible under the warm, olive tone of his skin, which felt just as thin as it had before, like it couldn't contain all of him.

There were things about yourself you could change, I thought. Trimming and trimming at the wheel. There were ways you could cultivate a self that looked and sounded the way you wanted it to, and it was easier, as it always was, to see it happen in other people. Especially after a long time. But when everything was stripped away, it was those things intrinsic to who we were, that we had developed before we were able to turn around and see ourselves as changeable, those things that remained. Seeing him like this, naked, the blood in his chest and cheeks, the trail of dark hairs beneath his navel, and the way he still shook like a leaf when he was excited—I felt a tenderness for him, and I knew the young person I once loved lived inside this man. Then he folded me in half beneath him, my ankle hooked above his shoulder, and I stopped having thoughts.

After, I sat in his bed, leaning against the headboard, drinking a glass of water. The music was still playing, and I wondered again at how long he had worked to make it so seamless. When I asked, he laughed.

You would notice that, he said. Analyzing everything, all the time.

I don't do that, I said, but he was right, I did.

You'd get that look on your face, he said, when something wasn't quite right at a party. Even when you were falling-on-your-feet drunk. Your eyes would narrow, and you'd scan the environment until you figured out what was going on. That someone's ex had walked in but no one else had noticed, something like that. Or, he

said, touching my elbow, it was the look you got when you were deciding whether you wanted to go home.

Mm, I said. I didn't want to think about going home.

A silence rose up between us, and I moved toward him, so that we
were touching again and I could feel the heat of his body against mine.
Is this what you do now? I teased, recovering. I put my chin on his
shoulder. Take girls home and seduce them with your sound system?

I wanted to make it nice for myself, he said, but yes, it helps. I set
it up when I first moved in. I told you, I have a lot of free time now
that I'm not a drunk.

I wake and I feel no pain, I intoned. I'm sure being sober has been
great for you, I said, but it's also made you weird and annoying.

When he laughed again I could feel it in his chest.

I'm still that person I was, he said.

Are you? I asked.

Yeah, he said. At night.

The walls come down, I said.

Yeah, he said again.

And your clay becomes soft again.

What?

Never mind, I said.

Colin was slouched against the headboard, and I slid down so that
I could rest my head on him, on that triangular plane where collar-
bone and chest and shoulder meet. We sat there, quietly, for a while.
Not long. I could feel his fingers tracing through my hair.

It's helpful to have a story I can return to, he said. I know it sounds
stupid.

It makes you sound like a serial killer, I said, and then I remembered that we didn't really know each other like that anymore, and

that what he had accomplished was deeply significant to him. I know what you're saying, I said. Sorry. I didn't mean to be mean.

It's helpful to declare those things about myself, he said. The things that are good, the things that I've gained. Otherwise, that whole experience, my whole reason for changing my life, becomes a black box. It's too painful, and I can't go in there.

His fingers drifted behind the shell of my ear and came to rest on my bare shoulder.

I'm sorry, I said again.

Do you feel that I've become boring? he asked me.

Not boring, I said. Something else.

I closed my eyes. When we weren't speaking, his presence felt the way he felt back then. The smell of his body and the warmth of his skin. But maybe, I thought, that was itself an imagined memory. The way I felt now was how I'd always wished to feel with him—sober, content, awake. I didn't think we had ever been so at peace before. If we had managed it, maybe we would have stayed together, and we wouldn't have become the people we became.

What was your story about us? I asked.

Hmm, he said. I think I thought of myself as a failure. His fingertips traced along my clavicle. When we met I'd gotten rejected from every PhD program I applied to, he said. Everyone told me to take a year off, and I decided to spend that year—well. You know. And I was happy in that failure, and I was having a lot of fun, but I was one. And when we met, I thought you were so pretty—

Aw—

—and smart, he said, and he knew I was going to say something cutting because then he added, I mean that, and in response I held my tongue.

And we were both still finding our way in the city, he said. I don't know if you saw it that way then, but I always thought of myself as following your example. Especially when you started to write. You were always more ambitious than I was.

I'm not ambitious now, I said.

You just wrote a book.

That wasn't ambition, I said honestly. That was something else.

I saw the new expression he had developed appear on his face. That expression of calm, patient waiting. I knew he was waiting for me to share more, to tell a story back.

But I wasn't ready to talk about my book with him, or how it had come to be, and I knew he wouldn't push me unless I asked. Let's have sex again, I said, because I did want that, almost desperately I wanted it, and I put my mouth on his mouth and touched him where I knew he liked to be touched, and that was the same as it had always been, that place and his reaction, and when it was done, I said, Let's go to sleep. Even though it wasn't that late. I wasn't tired, not physically, but I couldn't think enough to talk anymore. All our past selves seemed to be in bed with us, filling the room.

He fell asleep immediately, which I attributed to his sobriety. I lay awake for a while, listening to him breathe, thinking about the book event I had tomorrow, and what questions I might be asked, and what dress I would wear. I wondered what dream Colin would have, and if he would tell me about it when he remembered it in the morning, because when he said he remembered each one of his dreams I did believe him, and then sleep came for me, as it does for everyone eventually.

In the morning he asked if there was anything I wanted to do. Through the long picture window that spanned the length of his living room I could see the white arch of the Fremont and the rolling green-gray mass of the river. The sky was a pristine blue. I had woken to another missed call. Colin didn't tell me about his dreams.

I'd go to a museum, I said. Then I need to go back to my hotel and change. Before my reading.

Do you want me to come to that?

You don't have to, I said.

When I was a teenager I had worked as a docent in the contemporary wing of the art museum. I was an only child; my parents were quiet people who largely kept to themselves, and though neither of them would have admitted it, then or now, they were wary of the outside world. But it was this glittering outside world, full of pleasures and sights and sensations, that I craved, and after a tearful fight with my mother, I was allowed to take the job at the museum. The collection included a Helen Frankenthaler painting that I remembered loving when I first saw it: its wild abstraction, its presence on the wall proof that an important woman artist had lived and worked. During the two summers I worked in the contemporary galleries, the two summers before I left for college, I spent each morning walking in long rectangles, listening to the faint noise of video art emanating from the higher floors.

I should, I thought, see my mother. While I was here. But I hadn't told her the book existed because I was afraid of what she would say about it, and about what it said about me.

Let's go to the museum, I said. It's not a long walk.

The Frankenthaler painting was smaller than I had recalled it being. Less exciting. A stripe of pinkish paint streaked its way horizontally across the canvas, limned with a brown brushstroke that followed its underbelly. The pink paint dribbled and bled on the left side, forming a feathery blot. The top of the canvas and the right corner looked as though they had been dipped in dark green paint, which fanned and spread down the right side of the painting. But aside from these two motifs, nearly the entirety of the canvas was untreated empty space.

I remember it being bigger, I said. And more interesting.

It's not one of her best, Colin said.

There is something, I said, about the audacity of leaving all that blank space.

I felt around for more words but couldn't think of anything intelligent to say. I was disappointed that my memory hadn't served me. Though I'd spent the last day trying to avoid it in this town that had once held so much for me, I was there again, in that yellowish place of nostalgia, the color of things once aged. Even the canvas wouldn't have looked like this, I thought, when Frankenthaler first mixed her paints.

I was seized then by a sudden desire to see the painting as it had looked the day she made it. But I knew that was impossible. Even if a photograph existed from that moment, it too would have changed.

Was there ever a way to keep things just as they were even as they ended? To feel the pierce of first experience again, not because the puncture itself was repeated but because the memory could be stored somewhere, and accessed, and never changed? Or were we doomed to always choke our own histories with sentiment or regret—to flatten them into narrative, like Colin's black box of his sobriety, or my own book, which I was going to have to read from tonight.

He stood beside me now, his hands loosely clasped behind his back.

Your relationship, he began. You seemed sad when you mentioned it.

I'm not sad, I said immediately.

Okay, he said.

We began walking back through the contemporary wing to the main building of the museum.

I'm not sad, I repeated. But, I said, I did think I had it all figured out. A thread had come loose on the cuff of my jacket, and I pulled at it until it snapped.

When things ended, I said, I felt pretty foolish. That I had spent so much time with this person, whom I did love, and it still didn't work out.

It's not a crime that things end, Colin said.

Sure, I said. I just.

Then I felt like crying, and I was confused, because I hadn't expected it to happen here, and almost certainly not while talking to him.

I just thought that was the way to choose your own happiness, I said. That it was to choose it, I mean. To commit to something. And I chose that life, and it ended, and does it mean now that I'm bad at knowing what makes me happy?

Colin opened his mouth, and I stopped him, putting my hand out as if pushing something away.

Don't answer that, I said.

I wasn't going to, he said.

Frankenthaler, I said. Her first paintings were made with oils. She thinned the paint and poured it straight onto raw canvas. Because the canvas was unprimed, after a few years, the oil paint ate right through. They became degraded versions of themselves. She must have known it was going to happen, but for a while she made them anyway.

It's fine that it hurts, Colin said.

But what's the point of making something that isn't designed to last?

If I regretted everything I did before I got sober, I wouldn't have enough left of my life to call myself a person, he said.

He didn't touch me then, and I didn't want him to. I heard a far-off conversation bouncing to where we stood, the sound refracting off the white walls of the museum. Someone exclaimed; I couldn't tell whether with anger or delight. Someone else laughed.

There was a moment when I could have told Colin about what happened in P———. We'd unexpectedly spent a weekend together, about three months into our relationship. The constant contact brought us into a soft, tender relation, not our usual mask of irony and jokes, and Colin had been especially boyfriend-like that day, his touch lingering around my shoulders and waist. As night descended we had been in his room, drinking and talking, when he mentioned he still didn't know the reason I had moved to New York. Why had I come here, he asked.

I could have told him then. How I hadn't come so much as I'd needed to leave a different place. In that moment he might have been able to understand it, that story about me I had told no one else. But I didn't really know him then, and he didn't know me, and there was this new self I was becoming, a woman who had left her past behind, a woman whom I wanted desperately to meet. I was invested in that new self, in her coolness and invulnerability, and I wanted Colin to know me as that person. So I evaded the question. I didn't tell him.

In a way, I thought, I'd also become hardened. I'd trimmed my shape too, until I became refined, and sharp, and crystalline. The difference was that I'd done it before we met.

You don't have to regret anything, I told him honestly.

What was the core pain of nostalgia—that it wasn't true, or that it didn't last? Being with Colin in the city where I grew up, in the place where I had only ever been young, was like holding two tinted lenses up to a light. The colors of each were so strong they nearly kept me from seeing what was in front of me, which was Colin himself, his veined hands and forearms that I had kissed, thin-skinned, changed.

I'm trying not to, he said.

We started walking again. We were coming to the end of the museum's route; soon we would reach where we had entered the building.

Did you ever want to get back together? I asked him. After we broke up.

Yeah, he said. I missed you a lot my first winter at MIT.

Because it was cold, I said, stupidly.

He shook his head. Because you knew me, he said. Though it did snow a lot that year. You were one of the only people in the world who really knew what I was like, I mean. Maybe you didn't know that, but I thought about it a lot then.

And I hadn't known. I hadn't missed him; I had hardly thought of him. I had been entirely focused on what I was trying to accomplish, the transformation I was pulling, like a magician's silk, across my life, my past disappearing in its wake.

We were in the lobby of the museum, now. I stood with Colin, looking at him, really looking at him, willing this new version of him to join the old him in my head, the one I had kept trying to resurrect.

I didn't realize, I said.

It's in the past now, he answered.

Outside the museum, it was bright, the kind of day that makes all interiors feel like night. I blinked quickly, letting my eyes adjust as we stepped into the sun.

A crash. Shattered glass. He shouts at her. The artist has hurled a book at him—flutter of pages in the air, a bird's wings. It's missed him, taken out his wineglass. Red blots the pages and puddles on the floor. She hates him. She cannot stand him. She curses at him. He yells back. Calls her names. Her shoulders rise as she lunges. But doesn't touch him, falls just short of touching him. He leaves the room. She paces back and forth. As if over a kill. He returns with a rag. Wipes up the mess. She stops pacing. Enjoying the sight of him kneeling before her.

KATZ

n the novel I killed him.

In the novel.

In the novel the protagonist, who is based on me, kills the man, the older man, the artist, the old painter, who is more or less the professor I had once had, altering some biographical details.

I had not set out to write a scene of such violence. What I had set out to do was describe, in emotionally if not factually true terms, what happened. That was the process by which I wrote the book. The text itself elided the act of killing but the scene remained violent. While I was writing a trancelike state descended over me, which rarely happened when I wrote, and which I didn't question in this instance, even though I had always seen writing, unlike painting, as an act during which I remained entirely in control. After I wrote the scene, I realized that the book couldn't end any other way. When I was trying to sell the novel, a few editors remarked that they had been surprised by my character's decision.

She had run out of options, I thought.

Sure, it makes sense, one editor said, but it feels unearned. I just don't know if this character would really have the fortitude to do such a thing.

It was noon and I was at an all-day café attached to the lobby of a hotel downtown, my laptop out, pretending to work. I had arrived in Los Angeles early in the morning, catching the first flight out after my reading.

I opened a tab on my browser, started typing in the search field, changed my mind, closed it. Opened my email, scrolled down, very far down, hovered over the email from the old painter. Opened it, closed it. Then I sat, thumbs resting on the space bar, waiting for a thought to come.

I never read from the part where I kill him, or rather, from the part in which I, that is, she, the character, has a confrontation with him and after which it is implied that he is dead. I preferred to read from a scene at the beginning of the book, a scene that starts with the protagonist in her studio, a studio in a building that she shares with several other artists. She's immersed in her work, preparing the surface of a canvas. She's stretched it on wooden bars, stapled it down. It's a physical process—the pressure of the staple gun hurts her hand. She winces, shakes out her wrist, but she keeps going. After, the canvas is taut and ready to be primed. She goes over it once, twice, with gesso, letting it dry after each coat. While she waits for it to dry she looks at the ceiling, not thinking about anything. In between coats, she polishes the surface with a wet sanding sponge, creating a finish as smooth as printer paper. This takes hours. In writing the scene, I had lingered on the process, devoting pages to the repetitive, soothing motions of polishing the surface clean. After the canvas is ready—ordinarily it would take at least a day or two to dry, but in a novel, time can be manipulated—she stands at the easel, brush in hand, preparing to make the first mark. Her hand hovers above the canvas. The brush tip flexible, trembling, honest, ready. Then the painter walks in and her life changes.

That part was true. My life did change.

My phone buzzed. It was Frances. *Sorry, I'm running late,* she texted. We had plans to meet for lunch and then go to a few galleries on the west side. At one point in our lives, I might have stayed with her on a trip such as this, but I wasn't certain where we stood now, or if we were even still friends. It had been years since we'd seen each other in person, and almost as long since we'd last spoken.

Frances and I had met, fall of our freshman year, in the early-morning section of an introductory drawing class. We had bonded quickly over the unexpected workload, meeting in the common room of her dorm to work on the several drawings due each week. My style tended toward the gestural, the drawings smeared with marks from the various edges of a piece of charcoal; Frances's was precise, her work usually rendered in graphite, with thin, exact lines. Somehow, though her drawings required such fine detail, she worked faster than anyone I had ever met, and turned in her assignments in neat stacks, her grayscale shading so regular and true to value that they resembled black-and-white photographs. Because we started in the same drawing class, we ended up frequently taking the same courses, and so for four years, Frances and I studied together as artists, side by side.

Nearly every instructor we worked with tried to break Frances of her style, but she never gave in. There was something vaguely racist about the way they spoke to her—that her work was too clean, too blank, too serene. Of course the paintings were formally good, but they were hermetic, instructors complained. Repetitive. Unfashionable, even. Still, everyone acknowledged what a talent she was. No one could paint like Frances; that was why it was so galling that she continued to paint the way she did. When our classmates began to experiment with overtly conceptual work, incorporating video and performance, Frances remained stubbornly devoted to her subject, faintly neutered paintings of Asian women holding props in unusual situations. A woman sitting on a bed holding a water-filled bag with a goldfish in it. A girl wearing a school uniform, cutting off another girl's dark braid with a long-handled pair of gardening shears.

It had served her well. Out of our entire cohort, only Frances was still painting. Two years out of school she had gone to the graduate program at Yale, where her work had been well received. Next followed a handful of group shows, and then her big break, a solo show at a gallery in Los Angeles. She moved there not long after; we'd never lived in the same city in adulthood. Now she was represented by a bigger gallery, and I'd heard from another former classmate that two blue-chip galleries were courting her. She was in two group shows this summer; another solo show, her third, would open in the fall.

It had never occurred to me when we first met that people would compare us. Of course, they did. To an outsider, we were alike enough that our differences could be elided, but between us, all we saw were our differences. I was messy and Frances was neat. I wore my hair down and she wore hers up in a bun. I was perpetually single and Frances had been with the same person since she was fifteen. In school she had been deeply private about her relationship and rarely talked about her partner, though I knew that after all these years they were still together, and that they had gotten married recently. The biggest difference between us: I changed my subject over and over, and Frances continued to paint the same thing. No—I had given the medium up altogether, and Frances was still painting.

My phone buzzed again. *Be there in fifteen, will you get us a table?*

Slowly, without any rush or commotion, I began to pack up my things.

Frances's face shimmered in the mirage of heat from the tabletop grill. It made her pretty, neat features look underwater. Since moving to California, she had cut her hair, and it swung in a perfectly straight bob that hovered just below her jawline. I wasn't surprised, as I had seen pictures on social media, and it had become a consistent part of her look. Contrary to her tightly maintained image online, sweat shone on her forehead, the way I knew it pricked at mine, and that was how I knew that Frances still considered me a close friend, even if that designation was an old one, and in this moment didn't feel entirely deserved. We had ordered lavishly: thinly sliced beef sirloin, a pearly slab of pork belly, marinated short rib kalbi. Frances commandeered the tongs, expertly sliding the cooked meat to the side of the grill. Fat sizzled. I knew the smell would stay in my hair for hours. As if reading my mind, Frances paused to put her hair in a ponytail with an elastic she wore on her wrist. The blunt ends of her hair, gathered together at the nape of her neck, looked like the rounded head of a mop brush.

We can drive out to the west side and see some galleries if that sounds good to you, she said. There's a ceramics show, that figurative painting group show, a video installation I've been wanting to see . . . there's always some traffic but it's fine if we don't get to everything.

She picked up the tongs again. Kalbi?

Thanks, I said as she deposited the meat onto my plate. She had mentioned the group show when I told her I was visiting; she had two pieces in it, alongside other, more famous artists, whose proximity, I knew, would increase her own value.

How's the work going? I said.

It's going well, she said. She flipped over the slice of pork belly— a fresh crackle and hiss from the grill—and set down the tongs. I'm mostly making new paintings for this show in the fall. I have a proper studio now, so I can work larger, which I'm excited about. Next year I'll be doing a residency abroad.

I asked where and she said Iceland, in a small village that hosted a few artists-in-residence each season. It hadn't been her first choice, especially not the winter session, when her surroundings would be largely dark, cold, and isolating. But it was the session that the residency committee had offered, and she liked the idea of starting the new year somewhere completely different. In December she planned to ship her supplies to a neighboring village, where a team of craftsmen she'd been put in touch with would prepare her canvases. Come January she would be living in a cottage with minimal utilities and working in the nearby studio, located in a barn that she would share with a writer, a composer, and a dancer. It was unclear, she said, if the composer worked digitally, or if they played an instrument.

I knew that Frances usually worked while wearing noise-canceling headphones. It made it impossible to get her attention when she was in the zone; in the studio, I was afraid to tap her shoulder for fear of startling her and causing her to make a mark she hadn't intended to make. I had learned, during our last year in school together, to sidle into her peripheral vision, moving my body a lot, so that she would see me and set down her brush.

Either way, the sound shouldn't be a problem for you, right, I said, cupping one hand over my ear to mimic the shape of head-phones.

You remembered, she said, and I felt a flare of the closeness we had once shared. But it was weaker than I recalled, a flicker of the original feeling. What had originally enflamed it, what made it so hot and bright, was the competition we had been thrust into, the competition we had engaged in, a competition I always lost—until I finally won. When I went to her studio sometimes it was to ask her opinion of a choice I'd made, or to borrow some tool or medium she had that I didn't, but more frequently it was just to say hello—to see her guard slip, and for her to show herself to me. I didn't mind losing to Frances, not in the way that people outside of our friendship might have thought. I didn't care that she was the better painter, that she was awarded fellowships that sent her to Florence and Rome. What bothered me was that everyone pitted us against each other because they thought we were the same, when in reality we were completely different. It was a difference that made us hate each other as much as we loved each other, though I was never certain if that was because we wanted to be more similar, or if we couldn't stand that we weren't.

When I won the departmental award our senior year, I told everyone I thought it should have gone to Frances.

But to Frances I said nothing, because after I won the award, with its recognition, and its validation, and its lump sum, weeks before we were all to graduate and depart to different parts of the country, she stopped speaking to me.

Now she was saying that she was looking forward to the residency because the session was three women and one person, the composer, who identified as nonbinary. It was a relief when she received the bios of the other participants, she said.

You know how it is at residencies, she said, and I nodded, though

I didn't. All the writing I'd ever done had been conducted in coffee shops or on the tiny desk in the living room of my apartment, which, I realized, I had now been away from for just over a week. Somehow it felt like more time had passed. You know, she said again, all that forced intimacy.

She had a done a residency, a fellowship actually, in southern Europe, and the weather had been gorgeous the whole time, balmy, et cetera, but she had hated the man with whom she was forced to share a workspace.

I don't know when he slept, Frances said. He was there when I got to the studio in the morning and he was there when I left. The point of the residency was to foster interdisciplinary collaboration, she continued, but what it really meant was that there was always someone poking their head into her studio, even though she wore her headphones so that people would know not to bother her.

Right, I said.

This guy, she said, shaking her head, splaying her hands in frustration, he was so needy, he always had a question, he always wanted to know about my process, and then when I demurred he'd say, Oh, bellissima, you're busy, I understand, and he would make himself so pathetic, and then—for some reason—I would take pity on him, and I would explain to him what I was doing, and he would ask the right questions, and then just when I thought perhaps we were able to have a normal conversation and it wasn't so bad, he would say the crudest, dumbest thing, like banging two pipes together, absolutely Neanderthalian, and I would realize I was dealing with a fool, a fool who had somehow conned the government into paying for him to hassle me.

Why did you keep letting him into your studio, I asked.

I don't know, Frances said. It wasn't every day. It wasn't every time. At dinner, I saw him have conversations with other people that were charming and natural. People liked him. He wasn't actually a fool, I don't think. But for some reason, he insisted on showing that part of himself to me. Reveled in it, even.

I wasn't surprised that Frances had allowed such behavior to continue. She seemed hard, and she looked hard, but it was that exterior hardness she relied on to keep people away. If you were bold enough, or maybe stupid enough, to try to break past that exterior, it dissipated, revealing someone who had trouble driving out that which was unwanted. In school she had never had many close friends, and I recalled being surprised by whom she chose to surround herself with. I wondered now if she hadn't really chosen them at all.

Once, I remembered, she had called me in the middle of the night, nearly in tears, asking if I would help her get a bird out of her apartment. I had been at a party but I answered the phone, showed up a little tipsy and carrying half a bottle of wine. At first I couldn't find the bird, but then we heard it, the frantic flutter of its wings, and I chased it around Frances's apartment while she giggled helplessly. It was small—a house finch, a sparrow?—and it kept eluding my grasp, and finally we were reduced to looking up its removal online. One website advised turning off every electric light and opening a window. The lighter, different category of darkness from outside, the velvet smell of the air, the freshness of the leafing trees, would draw the bird out. So the website promised. We were skeptical, but we did as instructed, and within a minute, maybe two, the bird sailed out of the window and into the night. Frances pulled the window shut, and we hugged each other, triumphant.

It would have been nice if that moment had brought us closer together. If I had stayed; if she had asked me to stay; if we had sat on the floor together, talking. But I went back to the party not long after, and Frances kept doing whatever she had been doing in her room.

A college friend once asked me if Frances and I had ever been in love. With each other, they meant. No, I said, almost instantly, and it wasn't a response born of denial but a response of certain knowledge. We spent a lot of time together. We did things for each other. When we worked late in the studio, Frances brought me tea and sandwiches from the deli across the street without ever being asked. She proof-read my artist statement. We helped each other stretch canvases, took turns with the stapler. And I—I protected her. In school, she'd been passive at times, almost to the point of meekness; other times, she'd been unusually blunt in social situations and during critique. I had advocated for her, defended her, explained her to other people. But outside the intensity of the studio, our relationship had always been tightly circumscribed.

Once, Frances had asked me to model for her. She wanted to try something new, in the small, incremental way that she did. Previously she had always used photos for reference, and her figures did have a flat, paper-doll quality that lately our professors had been challenging. We reserved a classroom and locked the door and I stripped and stood where she asked me to. Then she studied my naked body in a matter-of-fact, clinical way. She had a list of poses she wanted, which I understood would be reference material for her paintings. I sat for perhaps two hours, all told. We didn't talk much, except for when she asked me to adjust something: the tilt of my hip, the position of my hand. Each time I changed position, she asked if I was comfortable, and she worked quickly, using only rudimentary shading. In the fin-ished work that resulted from the drawing session, her figures looked more solid, jointed, like they would cast shadows. I became a woman reclining on an analyst's couch. A woman crouching underwater. Two women, holding each other by the shoulders. I couldn't recall doing that pose—I wouldn't have been able to hold it long enough for her to draw me like that, not without a place to rest my hands—but I recognized the shape of the torso beneath the clothes, and I knew anyone who knew me would see it too. I didn't know when Frances had had time to memorize my body. Did she learn it all in that instant, or had she always been watching?

As close as we had been, it was hard not to treat Frances with caution. Even after all this time, I wasn't really certain what she wanted, or if she wanted anything.

Anyway, Frances said. I did end up making some work, at the end of the session. I became nocturnal, and I painted without any natural light. The colors didn't make any sense, and the figures grew all weird and elongated. I called it the nightmare series. They sold okay, she said. I wouldn't do it again.

In the novel there was no possibility of love. In the novel there was no possibility of forgiveness. My story had become, in my mind, the only story there was.

The narrative, which I had maintained for nearly ten years now, was that I had had to make him a villain in order to move on with my life. Writing the book had felt necessary, too, like an exorcism. It had started close to truth and then diverged broadly from fact at distinct points. I made the gap in the characters' ages larger. Made the old painter crueler. Made myself—the protagonist—prouder, and with more artistic potential to lose. In the novel I made them fight more, architecturally, baroquely, when in real life we had hardly clashed; it was I who always acquiesced to his demands. At a certain point the book stopped being an exorcism and became a project of craft and form. Then I grew totally absorbed in the writing, in the tuning and pitching, bleaching event into fiction. But it had always come from life; the life it came from was mine.

So why was it that I seemed to have forgotten he was a real person at all?

As if some part of me realized this, when I arrived in L.A. with time to kill I had intended to work, but instead, following a stray link from an arts magazine's newsletter, I started reading articles about the old painter, studying the pictures that appeared. I knew from knowing him that the portraits the papers used were at least ten if not fifteen years old. I told myself that as long as I didn't type his name into the field of the search engine I wasn't being weird. And even if I did, it was information.

He was not married. He lived in New England, possibly Maine. He did not have children. He probably looked the same as I remembered. Grayer, maybe, with those raptor's eyes. And a new paunch, a softness around his middle. Or maybe he was one of those men who grew leaner as they aged, cheekbones cutting through the fat.

I thought about the email again. *That's not how I remember it.*

He knew, then, that there was a version of me that killed him.

One of Frances's paintings in the show was in the entryway of the gallery, a small work that greeted visitors as they passed through. The second, larger painting was with the other works and hung opposite an Alex Katz. It was a departure for her in that it featured three figures, where usually in her work the women stood alone or in pairs. One girl lay on the ground, her body translucent, the background visible through her skin. Another girl crouched over her, hands gently cradling either side of the first girl's head. A third stood at the transparent girl's feet, looking down at both figures. The transparent girl was nude; the other two wore simple historical garments that made them look nearly allegorical. All three of the figures had long dark hair, the darkest parts of the painting. As in most of Frances's paintings, the figures loosely floated in space, against a light pastel ground that suggested neither interior nor exterior but a third, dream field.

The painting was beautiful: the technicality of it, the way the strokes had been laid down. It was a pleasure to see the image unfold, to move up close and see it break into gesture, then step back and see how neatly everything fell into place. The colors had an unusual clarity and were not muddied at all but shone, precisely, and I knew that Frances had carefully mixed and selected each one. The figures, especially the translucent one, seemed to glow, and after standing together for a few moments, I told Frances as much.

Thanks, she said, it was fun to paint.

She had been curious about how it would feel to paint a translucent figure, and wondered if she could pull it off. Did I notice—she pointed to a part of the canvas—there was some white mixed in, those little kinetic strokes, to give it the sense of being made of light, and not just a transparent, solid object.

Yes, I said, I did notice that.

It took me a while to figure out, Frances said. That's something I love about painting. There are some things that are easy and I do them all the time. And there are things that are hard that I try to do. And there are things that are hard that I'll never do again.

Was this easy or was it hard?

It was appropriately hard, I think. I want to do it again, she said.

As much as I admired it, I had always been simultaneously perplexed and intrigued by Frances's work. It never changed. She always painted women, and always the same kind of woman: Asian, like us, with thick, dark hair. The tenor of the paintings was always the same, too—a kind of quiet, hermetic mysticism, edged here and there by the presence of some cultural symbol that gave the work a jaggedness while skirting any outright accusation of Orientalism. I had never liked that, in college, some of her figures wore Japanese schoolgirl uniforms. It felt too easy, and appropriative in a weird way, as if she were banking on the fact that to white people, we all looked the same, no matter where we were actually from. The racial discomfort was part of the work—viewers were drawn in, then repelled, confused as to who was actually being tokenized and whether the desire they felt was coming from a mockery of that desire or if it was in fact earned. But in the larger scheme of things the paintings sold well, very well, probably at least partly because of the perceptions of Asian women Frances continued to evoke, and I wondered what she actually thought about it all. Was gaming the system by enacting the stereotype really gaming it? I didn't think most collectors were wise enough to know they were being played, and I wasn't convinced that Frances thought she was playing them. I was curious, too, as to how much she actually wanted to make these paintings.

I read her interviews and profiles whenever she shared them on social media, and in them she had touched on some of these themes. Her stance was feminist, insofar as painting beautiful women could be said to be feminist, and when asked, she delicately hinted at the notion of exploring and expanding depictions of Asian womanhood. But she never actually said much, and cultivated an air of mystery, and many of the articles featured photographs of her, standing straight-backed in her studio, wearing something black with an interesting silhouette, looking, as always, terribly beautiful, too.

How's David doing, I asked, turning to look at the Katz. A man,

seen from the back, sitting on a beach. Four figures behind him, all in
a state of repose. The rendering of it sleek, streamlined, insouciant.
David was Frances's husband. They had met in high school. He was
an architect, though not a famous or fashionable one. I had never met
him, though I had seen photographs. He was handsome, with straight
black eyebrows.

He's well, Frances said, he's working a lot. As usual.

Congratulations, by the way, I said. On getting married.

Frances shrugged. It felt like it was time, mostly to please our parents. Also because they were upset we're not having children.

You don't want kids?

No, Frances said. The way we were standing in the gallery, side
by side, a few feet apart, I couldn't see her face. We decided not to, she
said.

Before I could respond she moved closer, turning toward me, becoming legible again. Whatever expression had been on her face was
gone now, if there had been anything, and instead she was looking
at me.

Speaking of congratulations. I read your book.

I felt caught. In the same way I had never imagined the old painter
would read it, I'd never thought someone like Frances would read it
either.

Thanks, I said. I— And then I wasn't sure what else I wanted to
say. Heat flared into my cheeks.

It's good, she said, as though she had not noticed my discomfort.
It's really well written. It's intense, she said, and I knew that even
though I had not told her anything, she knew, or had inferred, what
had happened.

Thanks, I said again.

I noticed something, she said.

I didn't know how to reply, so I lifted my hands, tucked my hair behind my ears, and then placed my hands at my sides again, waiting for her to continue.

The character you wrote never actually paints anything, Frances said. She's trying to make something, but she's constantly getting interrupted. The book opens with her preparing her surfaces, and there are all these scenes set in her studio. But what does she actually make?

Well, I said. This close, I could see her long, straight lashes, the shimmery crease of her double eyelids. I looked over at the Katz painting. One of the figures, a woman, was reading. The book's cover was mimetically rendered, but from this distance I couldn't make out what it said.

The book, I said. If you take it to be a first-person artifact.

Frances stared at me and then she turned so that we were again facing in the same direction, looking at the Katz. Sweeping lines, glossy, empty space. A bright, sunny day, and people idling.

I can't believe you're a writer now, she said.

Why not?

It's just— That's all we did for four years, together, wasn't it? Paint? I never thought you'd stop.

I'm a better writer than I am a painter, I said.

You're a lovely writer, she said. But that's not what I mean.

I'm not like you, Frances. I lacked discipline.

No, you didn't! She was angry, I realized, making small, forceful movements with her hands. I saw how hard you worked.

No, I said. When it really got hard, I gave up.

The white lights of the gallery were hot against my skin.

Isn't it painful? Frances asked. To abandon a medium. There are so many things I can't say any other way.

That was the difference between us, I said. You kept going, and I couldn't.

When I first met Frances we were both seventeen. I had bought the wrong kind of charcoal for an assignment—compressed instead of willow—and without being asked she broke a stick of hers in half and handed a piece to me. She was so young then; I could still picture her as she was on that first day, her narrow, thick-framed glasses, the unfashionable heaviness of her bangs. Thank you, I said, and then I said, I'm Christine. I know, she answered.

You should've won the award, I said now.

It was years ago.

Still. It should have been yours.

I did fine without it. I mean.

I kept my eyes fixed on the painting. The man's hair was haloed with flyaway strands, as though the figures were sitting in a breeze.

At the time, I said. It meant so much to me. Like a sign that art could be my life, my real life. I didn't believe that about myself, not the way you did.

Some months after I left the MFA program, Frances reached out. We had gone nearly a year without speaking by then. Without pre-amble, she asked how I was doing, how the work was going, and she shared that she had gotten into Yale. The knowledge that she would continue painting, at a prestigious program, whereas I had just quit, gutted me.

I had wanted badly to tell Frances what happened. She had been my first artist friend—maybe my only artist friend—and I had wanted her to grieve with me, or for me. But at the same time I was filled with shame, and afraid that she would intuit what I suspected was true about me: that I was a fraud with no talent, and that my body had been the only thing our professor wanted from me. If Frances knew even the contours of what happened, there would be no way for me to escape her penetrating gaze, and I couldn't bear to hear what she would say, or to anticipate how badly she might wound me. I didn't want to be known by her, and I couldn't imagine a world in which she wouldn't know me.

I never responded to her email, and as the years went by I continued to follow her work online. Not long before the pandemic, we ran into each other at a party in the city. I was shocked to see her, so thoroughly had I separated her and her social media presence from any reality that included mine. We greeted each other warmly, and talked some, though I retained none of our conversation. It had felt the entire time as though we were speaking through long, telescoping tubes, our words diminished and metallic by the time they reached the other's ears. Still, we made plans to meet again. A few weeks later, the world went into quarantine.

After everything that happened it became tainted, I said now. The thought that he might have had something to do with it. Put me up for it, maybe. Even pressured the department. I don't know, I said, and I hate that I don't know.

Did you really believe that? Frances asked.

When I didn't say anything, she continued, her voice quiet, neutral. You stopped painting because of him.

That's not, I said. That's not what happened.

But that was how that door closed and I had been the one to close it. I could have transferred to another program, could have taken a job as a studio assistant or rented a place somewhere in the city, paid for a place with a sink, and a wall, and a window. Not even a window. I could have worked with artificial light. Made the colors loose and strange. I had let that dream die instead, and in choosing to write a book about it, I had chosen revenge.

I wish you'd told me, Frances said.

I wanted to, I said. But I couldn't.

I would have listened, she said.

Maybe, I said, and she didn't say anything. But what if you had judged me, or said something cruel?

I wouldn't have been cruel, she said. Not knowingly. I would have helped you move, she said.

I emptied my entire studio, I said. I gave everything away. You would have judged me for that.

Yes, she answered, and I knew she was being honest even though it hurt her. I'm sorry. Yes. I would have.

I remembered then something else about Frances, something that I hadn't thought about since we had lived in the same city. It happened only a few times—no, less than that, only twice that I knew of during the years we were in school. The winter of our junior year she abruptly disappeared. Stopped showing up to class; stopped answering calls and texts. Four days after she first skipped class, I went to her apartment, and knocked on the door until she answered, opening the door just a crack. But I could see the place was a mess. Dirty dishes were stacked in the sink; the floor was barely visible beneath a layer of clothes and trash. Let me in, I said.

I can't, Frances said.

I'll help you, I said. I'll help you clean.

No, she said.

It's okay, I said.

No, she said again. I'll be fine. And she closed the door again, and when I knocked some more, she didn't answer. From the street below

I could see that her lights were on, and I stood outside for a while until they turned off. The next week Frances was back in class, her hair clean and shiny, like nothing at all had happened, and when I moved to ask her, she said, I don't want to talk about it.

The next time it happened, maybe a year later, when I went to her apartment, there was no response at all. I knew she was in there, and I knew what it looked like, and I wondered then what would have happened if I had gone in that first time, even though she had said no. If I had insisted on helping her. Would she have let me, and would it have changed anything.

Did it happen again that spring, after I won the prize we both thought Frances would win? It had hurt so much when she stopped talking to me that I avoided every place I thought I might see her. I wouldn't have known if she had disappeared.

It's okay that you're not painting, Frances said now. I don't judge you, if you're concerned.

Why does it mean so much to you? I said. I wanted to hurt her but I didn't know how. What I do, I said. What I don't do. Why do *you* keep doing it? My throat was dry; I swallowed but it didn't help. What does any of it matter, anyway, I said. What you and I do.

She turned away from me then, looking hard at the wall.

It doesn't matter, she said. But.

Do you ever think about how you're an animal? Underneath everything, she said. The clothes, car, job, relationships. You're supposed to do all the things an animal does. Breathe, shit, fuck, eat. And you're supposed to be happy about being alive. You're supposed to be glad you exist. But there's something wrong with me. I can't do those things, those things that seem to come so easily to all the other animals. Sometimes I can't move. Sometimes for days. Sometimes it feels like there's a voice in my head, a distorted, fucked-up voice that tells me it'd be easier if I didn't exist. But the only thing, the only thing that makes it stop, even just for a little bit, is the work. If I can prepare a canvas, I have something to work on for the next day. If I know what I'm painting, I can get out of bed. My brain turns into barbed wire if I don't work. I've learned that now. I don't want to go there again.

I knew if she looked at me, if she saw that I was listening, we would never speak again. I stood still, waiting.

I don't care about money, Frances said. Small tears were showing in her eyes. I don't care about being famous. Everything I do, everything I've done in my stupid little life, is so I can keep painting. It doesn't matter what it is. It's not about what's in it, it's about getting to make the thing at all. If it sells, I have a career, and if I have a career, I can do this. And if I do this, I don't—

She stopped speaking.

Want to die, I said.

Yeah.

I wanted very badly to touch her but I didn't.

When it happened I wanted to die, I said instead.

You didn't, though.

No, I said. I didn't.

In the car I felt like we'd both been crying. Frances kept sniffing and pushing her hair off her forehead. My mouth was dry, and I picked at the chapped dead skin on my lower lip until it bled, a thin red crease I could see in the side-view mirror. We had agreed, more or less silently, that gallery-hopping was over, and Frances said she would drop me off at the bookstore for my event that night. As she was merging lanes she cut off the car beside us, and at the red light, the driver pulled up alongside and rolled down his window.

Fucking Chinks can't drive, he spat. After a beat, her eyes on the walk signal, Frances rolled down both our windows.

Fuck you, we yelled, flinging our hands out in unison, middle fingers extended. Then the light turned green and she accelerated, leaving him behind.

I wanted to laugh, but none of it was funny. It didn't bring us closer together, but this time I hadn't thought it would. This was not the end of our friendship, I knew. But I understood that this was how it would be with Frances. This jagged, painful intimacy, both of us carrying the memory of the thing we had once shared. We were women now; we would never be able to unknow each other, or the girls we had been. We could no longer be those girls to each other, even though they moved between us, constantly, with a flashing of eyes, and hair, and teeth.

She parked and didn't undo her seatbelt. I opened the door and got out, then leaned back inside, one knee on the leather seat.

Frances, I said. But I wasn't sure what I was trying to say. Thanks for giving me a ride, I finally said.

Of course, she said. She reached out and touched my hand where I had braced it on the dashboard. Then I straightened and she lifted her hand from mine, and then she was gone.

I was early, so I had time to get a glass of water and prepare myself for the event. The bookstore filled slowly, and there were a few things I had to do—mic check, pronounce my name for the host, sign stock. By the time the event was about to begin I was fully in author mode, slightly anesthetized, and I gazed pleasantly into the middle distance as people filed in. There wasn't much seating, so the latecomers had to stand.

A man walked in as I was beginning to read, letting the door fall shut behind him. The noise of his entrance caught my attention, throwing me out of my rhythm. I paused, took a sip of water, glanced out at the audience. He was an older man, white, not very tall, his gray hair covered by a cap; he stood in the back of the bookstore, obscured by the others who had come late. I was certain it was the old painter: I had known that body before; surely I would know it again. The same way Frances had memorized my body all those years ago. But the lights of the store were bright in my eyes, and I couldn't make out the details of his face, and the old painter I had known didn't keep a beard, and never wore a hat, and was it possible that after my morning on the internet, gleaning every possible piece of information I could about him, I was seeing things that weren't there? I was in California. Far from where he had any right to be. I set down my glass of water, drew close to the mic, and kept reading. My mouth moving automatically, the words spilling out.

I would approach him, I thought, when I was done; I would see for myself. But there was a flurry of questions from the audience as soon as I finished, and I saw him leave before I could make my way through the crowd.

Sometimes, at night, she considers it. How she could do it. How it would feel. Her mind circles the idea, dizzily, each pass giving it heft and realness, until she can feel the weight of it, balanced like a knife in her hand.

MARTIN

═══

When I got back to my hotel that night I saw I'd received another email.

You should try reading a different section, one from later in the novel. Perhaps one with a bit of a frisson?

The man at my reading hadn't been him. I understood that. The old painter was wherever he was supposed to be—Massachusetts, Maine. But there were other ways he could have learned what passage I was reading, and here he was, telling me he had. My publisher had made a flyer of all my planned appearances, the book's cover prominently featured next to the author photo I had finally acquiesced to taking; on tour, I had left a paper trail of interviews and blog posts and video clips that I re-shared on my social media. I'd been indiscriminate about what I reposted: my Instagram story was a hyphenated, stop-motion string of publicity. When I checked to see who had viewed my posts from the last twenty-four hours, there was a cluster of burner accounts at the bottom of the list, all faceless, all nameless. Any one of them could have been the old painter. He knew where I was.

Hands shaking, I tapped through my own posts again, swiping past still photos to find the one video I'd re-shared from the reading. Someone had filmed it from the back of the bookstore, zoomed in so that each small movement of the camera was magnified and jerky. In it, I was centered tightly in the frame, my shoulders hunched over the podium; the angle was bad and unflattering. The video began partway through the reading, starting midsentence. When I flicked on the sound and heard my own voice, strained and tight and sounding nothing at all like the voice I heard in my head, I immediately swiped away. The next post was an ad, a blaring, thumping intrusion, and I swiped out of the app, muted my phone, and threw it on the hotel bed.

I hated how ugly and awkward I looked in the video, and I hated that he—the old painter—must have seen it. That his eyes were on me. What else of mine had he followed—what else did he know?

Alone in my hotel room, I shut my eyes tightly, breathing slowly through my nose. I was being ridiculous. I'd come this far. I couldn't go back.

I opened the app again and deleted my repost of the video. Then I felt stupid and paranoid for deleting it. I moved to share it again, changed my mind, closed out of the app, and for good measure deleted it off my phone.

The old painter's email played in my head. I could hear it in his voice.

One with a bit of a frisson?

In the book there was one scene that could be taken to be a moment of—I wouldn't call it love. No. Maybe infatuation. It appeared at the end of the first chapter; I usually only read from the opening pages of the novel. In the scene, the protagonist has just had a close, charged encounter with the old painter, a critique in which he has both praised and critically pierced her work. He has seen something within her, a specialness that she recognizes within herself. The gravity of his charisma and power has left her with a giddy exhilaration. Through his proximity, she feels that she has come closer to a great, true understanding of art. She feels noticed. As if her potential, which has been quietly glowing inside her, and in whose cultivation she has toiled daily, will now blossom and grant her all the rewards that creative labor entices us with. The scene takes place in her bathroom, at night, as she recalls the events of the day. Standing in front of her fogged-up mirror, slowly detangling her wet hair with a wide-tooth comb, she imagines the paintings she'll make. The fame she'll attain, the way her brush will move fluidly over the canvas, every mark the exact mark she intended. Her excitement is heady, drunken, bordering on sexual pleasure.

In my mind, the scene was a turning point, where the protagonist tips from curiosity into full-blown obsession. It's the moment in which she chooses to pursue him. Not, I thought, that she truly pursues him. The power differential between them doesn't allow for an honest pursuit. But she takes an action in that more sly and uncertain territory—she turns to face him, listening.

There's another scene the next day, an interstitial, a moment in her studio during which nothing much happens. Frances was right. My character never paints anything. The following evening, she encounters the old painter at a reception. There's wine; her stomach is empty. They've begun to circle each other: each now aware of what the other is doing.

There's no sex in the novel. I didn't want to write it. It felt gratu-itous, and I was afraid the book was already gratuitous, if in a banal way, because these things happened all the time, and had happened to me. The sex wasn't interesting; it hadn't been the most interesting thing at the time. That had been the future the old painter had shown to me—however briefly, however fantastical.

I'd changed the story when I wrote it down. Pitched it as high and piercing as it would go, a soprano's final aria. Made my character sharper, shallower, more aware of her powers than I had ever been. I'd gotten carried away. I could see that now. And I regretted it for what it said about me.

Surprising myself, I opened the email and wrote back.

Which section was your favorite?

Then I threw my phone on the bed again and, turning away so I could not see its dark face, I began to pack.

I was in Santa Fe the next afternoon, in a rental car to Taos by eve-ning, blinking hard at the road, my eyes dry from the hours spent on planes. I had wanted to make some stops on the drive up—I wanted especially to go to Ghost Ranch, to see O'Keeffe's studio—but the sun was setting. In the graying light, the unfamiliar landscape of mesas and sagebrush provoked an intense loneliness in me, and I sped into the evening, with no music playing, with no sound in the car at all.

I was house-sitting in Taos as a favor to a friend, who had con-nected me with a bookstore in town to do a reading. I had met Kristen at the arts administration job I worked after moving to the city, and when she decamped for the Southwest a few years later, we stayed in touch. Her home was a one-bedroom cottage not far from the center of town. She was having the floor of her kitchen redone while she was away; could I let the contractors in? Yes, I could.

When I arrived it was night. I found the key in a lockbox and let myself in. The house was small, one story with an open plan, the kitchen temporarily separated from the rest of the cottage by a wall of translucent plastic sheeting. I pulled the plastic back to look and saw the floor had been stripped and prepped, the new tiles waiting in neat stacks. A layer of dust, stirred up by the renovations, coated the bare floor and counters. The bedroom was set apart by a rounded archway through which the rest of the house was visible. I unpacked my things and lay on top of the bed, still fully clothed. I couldn't imagine buying a house, but somehow Kristen had, and it had taken her away from everyone we knew. She didn't seem to mind. It felt so good, she told me, to have a home that was just hers, where she could live a life she didn't have to explain to anyone.

I thought of my own apartment, imagining its floor plan. Made myself walk through its hallways and doors. It was strange to think that I had lived there for years. I couldn't afford it now. I'd have to move, I thought, when I got back.

Outside the darkness had turned syrupy and thick; I could just make out the silhouettes of pine trees against the sky. There wasn't much of a yard: The grass was bare in spots, overlaid with gravel in the driveway, and I had seen a clutch of aspen trees nearby when I pulled in. It was dark enough that I pulled the blinds closed, even though Kristen didn't have any neighbors close enough to see inside. With the lights on, the window felt too much like a mirror.

I took out my laptop and notebook, setting them on the desk in the bedroom. I had a vague fantasy of trying to write while here, perhaps even start a new project. Something different from the novel, which instead of being a unit for containment seemed to have swelled to encompass my present as well as my past. I wanted to become someone entirely new, without a history, without the tangled tail of event and consequence that dragged behind me. In the bathroom, I arranged my toiletries around the sink, the tube of toothpaste and cleanser and toner all doubled in the mirror. I looked terrible. My skin was breaking out; my hair was somehow both greasy and dry. I was traveling too much. I washed my face carefully, using lukewarm water, and took extra time to massage in moisturizer in small circles, using as little pressure as possible. I knew I needed to make changes soon.

From the bed, even lying down, I could see the ghostly outline of the half-finished kitchen. I couldn't see clearly through the plastic, only its grayish shape, and I kept thinking the sheeting would move, as if from a breeze. Its stillness perturbed me. I got out of bed and turned on the overhead light in the kitchen, thinking perhaps it would create a warm, diffuse glow, like a paper lantern, but it only created shadows, which I could see through the plastic, eerie and undefined. When I turned off the light it was still frightening, having created in myself the knowledge that such shadows existed, and so I took a table lamp from the living room and placed it on the counter, drawing the sheeting open so that I could see the bulb and its yellow light, and I fell asleep like that, on my side facing the kitchen, one arm raised above my head like I was preparing for a fight.

In the morning I woke with a nosebleed. There was a fresh red streak on the pillowcase, and when I touched my face with the back of my hand it came away wet. The blood flowing from my nose felt strangely loose, almost too fluid, but it stopped within a few minutes. It was the altitude, I knew; I felt hungover, even though I hadn't been drinking.

Outside, the sky was a blue so vivid every shape seemed to have a double outline. The contractors were supposed to come around nine. I found some ibuprofen under the bathroom sink and swallowed it, then went out to stand in front of Kristen's house, glass of water in hand, taking in the vastness of the sky, which had been intellectually known to me the previous day but was absolutely, impossibly apparent this morning.

At nine no one showed up; at nine-thirty, no one; at ten, no one; at ten-thirty, I texted Kristen and drove west to Ghost Ranch. There was no shade at all, and I flipped the sun visor of the rental car down. On either side of the road, the mesas rose and fell in staggering formations. I kept wanting to look sideways out the window, to try to follow the mesas' changing shapes, but every time I turned my head, the landscape was already somewhere different, sandstone and limestone streaking into red and white stripes. In the rearview mirror I saw there was just one other car on the road, a white sedan that trailed behind me, neither speeding up nor slowing down. When I slowed, experimentally, it didn't pass me, but slowed too, until it was only a few yards away. In the glare of the sun I couldn't see who the driver was, and I realized I didn't really want to know, and I slammed my foot on the gas, accelerating until the car was out of sight.

I had met my ex at a dinner party hosted by a friend of Kristen's whom I didn't know. It was two years after Colin and I broke up, and I hadn't dated much or seriously since. My ex and I were seated next to each other, and I introduced myself as a writer. He told me he was a graphic designer. I didn't know what that meant, so I asked him, and he said it was about seeing the understructure of how people saw the world. There was a secret, invisible grid that lay beneath everything, a rhyme scheme that encompassed plants and animals, cities and cars; his job was to align shapes to it, to make things look the way they should, and to do it so elegantly that no one noticed he had moved anything at all.

I didn't go home with him that night, which I thought was a good thing, because when I went home with people upon first meeting them it usually didn't last long. When he got my number from Kristen and asked me out a few days later, I said yes, appreciating his forthrightness, and then I did go home with him.

I didn't tell him I had been a painter. He knew me as a writer, and I didn't mind that he didn't read my work. After we moved in together, we filled our shared apartment with slim-spined books and oversize monographs and mid-century furniture we bought from a man off Craigslist. I loved the life I had with him, a life that seemed to have been created out of nothing, a life in which I had no past, only a future, one toward which it seemed we were jointly turned. At night, in bed, I lay next to him, imagining a grid placed over our figures, a delicate, open-meshed net, and I pictured how we might look to someone floating far above, so snug and tidy, aligned according to the invisible logic of the universe, a logic that he claimed to know, and one I willingly obeyed.

I felt blessed with him. Like I had escaped something. Like I had finally done things right, was living my life the way a person should.

But we fought about the novel. I had waited until the last possible moment to tell him about it, and when I finally did, he couldn't understand why I was so fixated on something from the deep past, something I had kept a secret from him. Writing the book, I had descended into a fugue state. I ignored my freelance work and rarely left the house. The writing process took only a few months, but I emerged from it altered, and when it became clear the book would be published and read by real people in the real world, I became the worst, most anxious version of myself. I feared that I would be misread; I feared that I had shared too much, even though all around me it seemed that women had come to similar realizations, that these things happened, and that they had happened to each of us. My anxieties invaded the space of our relationship, a space that proved to have a void in the middle of it, a void that I had willingly created.

What I don't understand, my ex had said, was why you never told me anything. If it was this important, you should have said something sooner.

I needed time to understand how important it was, I said.

I'm just really surprised by all this, he said.

But—I saw the sign for Ghost Ranch and the turn to the entrance was sooner than I expected; I wrenched the wheel and took it hard, kicking up a cloud of dust—what was also true was that in dropping down into the place I needed to be to write the book, I had pushed him away. I had not allowed him to be near me while I was there. I had not let him touch me, had not explained what it was that I was writing until the result became inevitable. I had never told him about the old painter, and though I didn't think I was keeping a secret, it had become one, a door I was holding shut that he never even knew existed. When I flung it open, not only to him but to the world, how could he not be surprised by what it revealed?

It cost ten dollars for a day pass, which covered admission to the museums and the grounds of the ranch. For an extra fee I could take a horseback tour or a guided walk that included a talk on the landscape paintings of Georgia O'Keeffe. Her house, I learned, was inaccessible to visitors but could be glimpsed from one of the trails. I checked my email, there was nothing, tugged the screen down to refresh it, still nothing. Just inside the welcome center, two women discussed the watercolor workshop they were attending in the afternoon.

Did you know, one of them said to the other, that O'Keeffe's husband never set foot in New Mexico?

Seeing Frances had left me feeling bruised. I knew well enough that we had become different people and that indeed we had been very different from the start, but it stung to see how dramatically our lives had diverged. She'd found a way to survive that made sense for her; even if I didn't like it, even if I thought it was cheap, and even if I didn't always think she seemed happy, I knew she was safe, secure, and loved. What did I have to name as my life? I'd been safe, too, until I ruined the neat fiction I'd been living in.

When I first came to it I'd seen writing as a mode of reinvention. It required so few materials, all of which I possessed. A word's relationship to its meaning was exact; I found solace in the black-and-white of letters. When I wrote something, and it entered the world, and people read it and thought it was good—that was pure. Writing didn't require my body, not the way painting had; in fact, writing asked me to absent my body, to forget it for long periods while I worked. Language was supposed to be my perfect transmission, my power, my mark. Working on the novel, I thought that by putting the events on the page I would be freed somehow. But something different happened. I killed the old painter only in my fiction; in the real world, both of us still lived, and could speak. I'd been too confident in my prose, had thought obliterating him once meant I'd never again have to face what happened between us. I had not prepared myself for the moment when what I thought I'd released turned, and began to chase me.

A shadow passed over my phone and I nearly dropped it. When I looked up I saw only the white belly of a hawk circling high into the sky. I'd become nervous since arriving in New Mexico. The air was thin and it felt like everything passed through. Until now I'd always had someone else nearby to ground me: Even though seeing Frances had been difficult, I had felt present with her, able to identify my own personality and desires from the way hers, so strong and sharply formed, moved against me. Here, I felt too porous, without likes or dislikes, as though the sun would bleach me of all color.

The two women's voices returned to me over the noise of my own thoughts.

Well, Maria would send him photographs from the ranch, the other woman was saying, and I listened carefully, though I didn't know who Maria was.

A photograph is nothing like the real thing, answered the first woman. Not here.

I'd kept thinking I was seeing the old painter in all the places he couldn't possibly be. At the airport, out of the corner of my eye. At the rental car agency. On the highway up to Taos. Even here, now, in the high desert, I kept thinking I would see him—wondering if that was in fact what I wanted. If I wanted him to find me.

Not here, the second woman agreed.

The paleontology museum was small and bright and smelled strongly of dust. Though there were exhibits at the periphery, all my attention was drawn to the huge block of excavated earth in the center of the building. It was massive, all in one piece, fenced off by a wooden armature. Atop the block, which had been carefully chipped away in parts, were instruments: two microscopes, suspended in a metal frame; soft brushes; hammers and chisels resting on sheaves of paper.

It looked as though someone had just been working on it and stepped out. I looked closely to see if I could find any fossils, but the block was mostly encased in a thick white layer of what looked like plaster or limestone, its surface impassive and illegible, and after a minute or two I realized I didn't know what a fossil looked like when it wasn't cleaned and displayed in a glass case, or even really what a fossil was at all.

There was no one else in the museum. From a placard I learned that the block of earth in the center of the building had been excavated from a site on the grounds, where paleontologists had found the remains of thousands of dinosaurs that had been killed in a flash flood. On the display there was a drawing of the dinosaur *Coelophysis:* slender, long-necked, long-legged, and hollow-boned. Its head was pointed, like a needle, and the strata of the desert were dense with its remains. The block was intended to be a display of working paleontology. If you carefully broke through the rock and sifted through the softer material with a brush, the fossils contained within could be revealed.

A fossil, the placard read, *isn't a bone embedded in stone, but in fact the deposits of minerals carried by groundwater that have crystallized in the shape of the cells of the original living creature.*

Not the bone, but the stone's memory of the bone. I wanted to touch the excavated earth, feel the fine soil, make a bowl of my fingers and scoop through it searching for arrowheads and teeth.

What is it that archaeologists do when they prepare for a dig? They make a grid over the earth in string.

I had just received a set of cover options to review when my ex asked me to tell him what had happened. The story, the real story, the one

I'd avoided telling. The sample covers were printed out and fanned across my desk like playing cards, and we had the conversation like that, the evidence of my guilt or something like it staring us both in the face. When it started to go badly, I wanted to turn the pages over, to hide the colors and shapes, but I'd already shown my hand.

You were in grad school, he said.

Yes.

How did it start?

I don't know, I said. Slowly.

I knew he wanted me to say more.

It was early in the term, I said. I knew him from undergrad. He'd been a professor there before he asked me to apply to the program. I was in a new city, so. I looked to him. The way your eyes go to a familiar face in a room. And I was—I was lonely, I didn't know my roommate very well, I'd just met her off a mailing list, and our apartment was far from where the other MFA students lived. So I spent a lot of time on campus. I went to all the talks at the art school, and was the last one at the receptions. Once cleanup started, I'd go back to my studio.

I think it was one of those times, I said. I was in the studio. It was late. He came in—I don't know if he saw me go up, or if he just wanted to see what we were up to. And he said—

Suddenly I didn't want to say it.

What did he say?

He said he could tell how hard I worked.

I could feel the hot shape of crying in my throat, like it would come out with my next words.

It felt good to hear that, I said. I swallowed hard. I had a bad first crit. I tried to make friends, to get to know people, but it was still early on, and people didn't know how to talk about my work. I felt really . . . I felt stuck. The paintings weren't turning out the way I saw them in my head. Even my thoughts didn't feel interesting. And I wondered if I was meant to be at the program at all. Like, was there something I was supposed to be doing with my life instead. And when he said that—

I felt stupid for phrasing it like this, but it was true, or it had been—

It gave me reason to stay, I said.

After that, I said. It was gradual. He was kind to me. He would bring me references to work from, a book or something, a postcard, sometimes a little thing for my studio. Once a set of Sennelier pastels. He was charming, I said, and smart, I know it's a cliché, but everyone wanted to talk to him at the receptions. He could be abrasive, he had plenty of detractors. But he had this magnetism, I said. It was good to be in his orbit, and he was fond of me. And he was kind to me, I said again, forgetting I had already said it. And I was drawn in.

But how did it start, my ex repeated, and I realized he was asking about sex.

I don't know, I said again, my voice strained. I can't tell you the point at which my professor decided he wanted to fuck me. Maybe it was when I agreed to apply to the program. Maybe it was when he saw how I had no friends after I moved. Maybe it was when I was seventeen, a freshman in college, and he walked past me as I was on my way to introductory drawing, and I didn't even notice him, and all along he was thinking, *That one.* I don't know.

But you did, my ex said, go along with all of it. You consented.

Sure, I said, acidly. Yes. Yes, I let him invite me to dinner. And at dinner, I drank a lot of wine. Yes. I liked feeling special.

When the old painter saw how lonely I was, he invited me to his house. He talked to me. Listened when I talked back. No one, I

thought, had spoken to me like that before. Like I was going to become. Like he knew I was going to become.

Being close to him, coming to know him—it had all been more
enticing than the fear of what could happen, and what did.

I am trying to understand you, he said. Don't be cruel.

I'm not being cruel, I said.

This is how I feel, he said. We're together for four years. You tell
me nothing about your time in grad school. You don't even tell me
you went. Then, you start working on a book. You refuse to tell me
about it—

I was working, I said.

And then when it's done, you finally show it to me. Only because
I ask. And it turns out that the text contains this massive secret, also
unknown to me, which, for some reason, you have decided to share
with the entire world.

I put my hands on both sides of my face and touched my temples.
I had to write it, I said. Not making it wasn't an option.

It's not that you made it, he said. It's that you didn't let me into it.
He paused. I didn't know you were capable of doing something like
this.

I knew he wanted me to respond. That he, or we, needed me to
apologize, to steer us back to what was familiar, what was us. But I
didn't have anything to say, and we remained there in silence until he
stood and left the room.

In my email I asked the designer to do another pass; I wanted
something quiet, I said, with less color.

What I wanted to know was, how did the paleontologists know where
in the soil things were buried? How could they be so certain that the

excavated block contained something to find? Or maybe that was the wrong question. Maybe the question was—if they knew, with each movement of the chisel, that something was hidden beneath it—how did they not break what they found?

It was afternoon and I hadn't eaten. I took out my phone, refreshing my email. Nothing.

My ex and I had spoken more about the book before we broke up. It was a slow, sad dance we insisted on seeing through to its end. The more he asked, the more I said things that upset him. He wanted the truth from me, but nothing I provided seemed true enough for him, and I knew the issue was that I'd stretched it, distorted it in making the thing that finally felt true enough to me but was not true to the facts of what had happened, and he couldn't bear that difference, the difference of not knowing, not understanding that the gap between truth and untruth didn't matter, that it was about how it felt, that it had changed me. We engaged in this charade for weeks, a month, and at the end of the month he told me that he was leaving me, and he had met someone.

And so I left the city because I wanted to know how a person should live, and I thought if I asked enough questions, I would eventually arrive at some answer. I spoke to everyone who spoke to me, and I had long conversations. I went where my itinerary told me to go, and I read at the places I had been told to read, and now I was in a room in the desert, surrounded by dead things.

I knew I should eat, even if the thought of food made me want to retch. There was a cafeteria on the grounds. Inside the canteen, there were only a few people, talking quietly in small groups, and after I arrived and ordered, no one sat near me. Still, I was on edge, shoulders raised, jumping every time I heard a noise, the clatter of dishes being set down, the squeak of chair legs across the floor. I stirred around the contents of my plate with my fork, taking small sips of water. Then I took my phone out, refreshing my email, my thumb tugging automatically, and there was a new message.

I like the part where she trashes his studio. Touché, no?

The section was toward the end of the book—nearly the climax. Maybe it was the climax. After an argument, while the old painter is sleeping, my character takes his keys and sneaks into his studio. She finds a palette scraper, the kind that has a razor blade snapped inside. It has a bright-pink plastic handle, the color of a child's toy. She tests it on the pad of her finger, drawing blood.

She starts by destroying unpainted canvases, slashing them in long diagonal lines. Sometimes three or four cuts to a canvas. The fabric sags off the wooden frame. There is still something sacred to her about the finished painting. The labor of it. She is not precious about her own work, but she hesitates with his, even though she is angry with him and wants to hurt him. As long as she destroys only the blank canvas, the damage she inflicts is merely financial. He is a wealthy man. He can buy more materials, hire a fleet of young art handlers to stretch and prepare his surfaces for him. So once she has shredded his white canvases, left them in ribbons, she turns to his paintings, which lean against the walls, some stacked in tall shelves. She has come too late to cause real harm: Most of his work has been packed and sent away for a show. She doesn't realize this, or perhaps it doesn't bother her that much of what she destroys is the rejects, the set-asides, the ones not deemed worthy of showing. She begins with a large canvas, one she's always hated, it's abstract, they're all abstract, she cuts through it in one long vertical movement, using her whole body, tearing it in half. It's harder than she thinks. The paint is not thick, but it fights the blade; her knuckles are scraped up from pressing against the rough texture of the binding medium. The flayed skin stands out on her hands, she's bleeding, but she keeps going, slashing at the paintings, when the scraper gets stuck in a thick impasto smear of oil paint she leaves it embedded, finds a palette knife, uses it to wrench through the rest of the way. She destroys his big paintings first, it takes her a while to learn how best to slice through them, shearing through the backside where the raw canvas provides the least resistance, a clean tooth for the blade to work against. She punches her foot through a painting, then separates it from the stretcher bars, it slumps to the floor like a skinned animal, head still raised. She slices through all the paintings, rifling through shelves and storage to find every last one, and when she is done she takes his glass palette in both hands, holding it high above her head, and drops it so that it shatters on the poured-concrete floor.

She is breathing heavily by the end, sweating, her knuckles raw, her shoulders aching, but the rest of the building is silent. No one has heard her; no one saw her come in. She only leaves his paints, in the tubes, untouched.

I had enjoyed writing the scene: the carnage, the heavy symbolism of her revenge. After she locks up the studio, she returns to his home, where he is still sleeping, and replaces the keys where she found them. She leaves as if she has only left for an early morning. When he finds the destruction, they don't speak for a week. Well—he barrages her with calls, with angry texts, with threatening messages, but she ignores him until he sends her one word. *Sorry.* Though she is the one who has undoubtedly wronged him. Then they meet for dinner. Then they begin seeing each other again.

I had ordered enchiladas at the canteen, asking for red and green chilies, and without noticing I had mixed the mass into an unappealing brown blob on my plate. I began to eat, mechanically, not tasting anything. So that was the old painter's favorite section. I had expected him to choose one of the more overtly erotic scenes, one in which his character is still mysterious, still desirable. But he picked the one in which he is brought to his knees. I was intrigued by what that said about him—that he was more interesting than I remembered, or that his reading of the text, at least, was more interesting than I thought. I still hated his French affectations, the blunt, chauvinistic way he spoke. That hadn't changed.

I'm surprised, I typed into my phone. Was I really going to do this? *That's a bit masochistic.* I sent it. Felt a flicker of what had first drawn me in.

Out of nowhere, a large group of students came into the canteen; the room filled with noise, a woman who must have been the trip chaperone calling across the din. Jackets were flung across the backs of chairs, backpacks thumped to the ground. One girl's coat slid to the floor and I picked it up and handed it to her.

Thanks, she said, looking startled, and turned away before I could say anything.

Another email notification.

New message. Subject line: *A conversation.*

I received another email that same afternoon, one from the bookstore in Taos, letting me know that my event had been canceled owing to a lack of registrations. They would still, they said, be happy for me to come in and sign copies. I said I would, but the idea of showing up and signing stock when clearly no one was interested felt more humiliating than the event being canceled in the first place. A few hours later I got a message from the arts venue in Houston. They were so sorry, but would I be able to reschedule my event? A conflict had come up, and they needed the space to entertain an important donor, whose needs, I inferred, took precedence over my novel.

It was fine, I wrote back, in fact, they could cancel. The events person responded with a mix of apology and relief. It was fine, I repeated in my email, my travel plans had changed.

I wrote to Kristen. If she needed me to, I would stay until she returned, but I was hoping to depart a day or two early; something had shifted in my tour schedule. I mentioned again that the contractors hadn't shown up and wondered if I should call.

I took a long shower that night. I had never been to Maine. I had a few vivid associations with the state: Marsden Hartley, fir trees, and a particular opaque shade of orangey red, which I realized was the color of either cooked lobster or a safety buoy. I used the shampoo that was in the bathroom, repeatedly lathering and rinsing my hair until it felt squeaky against my fingers. Kristen's was more fragrant than the shampoo I used at home, and left my hair smelling of cedar and rosemary. I soaped my body and scrubbed at my face, trying to rid myself of the gritty, dusty sensation I'd been feeling. After, my skin was pink as if I'd been scalded. Though I hadn't yet heard back from Kristen, I started packing up again, putting my laptop in my bag, returning my clothes to the carry-on. The plastic sheeting in the kitchen still unnerved me, how I couldn't fully see through it, and the way it dropped straight down without moving. But what would be worse—that it didn't move, or if it did.

When I looked closely at the sheeting, I realized what I had thought was a translucent piece of plastic was actually reinforced with a gray woven mesh, the squares perhaps an inch across.

I was reminded of a painting I'd seen years ago, on a trip upstate. We had gone, my ex and I, to a museum that was housed in an old factory, where the industrial windows let in enormous amounts of light. The museum's collection was small, and exhibits were often on view for several years. In the center galleries, taking up two rooms, was a series of Agnes Martin paintings, most of them the pastel-striped compositions I had encountered before, which invariably reminded me of children's clothes, or color-coded spreadsheets. But there was one painting that nearly didn't seem like a painting at all. It had a white ground, covered in a fine graphite grid. The lines were thin but unwavering, the grid completely regular, without accent or error. I stood in front of it for a long time, wondering first whether I should call it a painting or a drawing, and then why the difference mattered to me. When my ex came to find me, having already done his rounds, he asked what I saw in it, and I told him, and we stood in front of it a while longer. I saw from the checklist that it was titled *The Beach*, from 1964, and then we wondered together why it was called that—if it came from a memory of sand or water.

It was a happy memory of mine, that visit to the museum. I thought now—turning out the light, letting the darkness settle onto me like a blanket—that I had been truly myself on that day, without omission or elision, and that had made the trip an honest one, one I wouldn't rewrite now; we had loved each other then, and it had been me he had loved, not some other person, not someone I was trying to be.

II

MAINE

take a morning flight to Dallas; from there, one to Portland, Maine. From there I take a bus to Rockport, and from Rockport I'm to take a ferry to a small island, one I wouldn't be able to identify on a map. To make sure I don't get on the wrong boat, I repeat the name of the island to myself over and over, under my breath, but when I get to the terminal on the mainland, I see that everything is clearly organized and easy to navigate. In the waiting area, a teenager in a tie-dye hoodie, lank brown hair falling over one eye, is napping on one of the benches, which resemble church pews. The ferry ride is beautiful, breathtaking; I can't stop watching the churning of the blue-green water as it streams away from the hull of the ship. The silhouettes of the other islands we pass, fringed with trees. I keep looking while the sky dims, until the sun has nearly set and I can't tell the difference between the sky and the water.

On the other side he is waiting for me. It's seemed like it's going to rain all day but it hasn't.

The old painter is wearing a light-colored windbreaker. No hat. He carries nothing. I have been outside for the entirety of the ferry ride, I wanted to feel the air on my face, and so everything of me feels the same temperature as the air, which is chilled. He takes my suitcase from me without being asked, I wouldn't have asked, and places it in the trunk of a car I don't recognize. It feels unreal that just hours ago I was in Taos, in the mountains. And now I'm in Maine.

The old painter opens the passenger door for me and I get in. He looks at me.

It's dusk now, the time of day when everything takes on the same value and I begin to feel as though my vision is failing. I don't know what expression is on my face.

I didn't think you'd come, he says.

His voice is the same. It bounces around my body, jarring loose the memories of its prior self. The way he used to tease me. The way he said my name. This isn't the first time he's waited for me to arrive somewhere; this isn't the first time I have come to him.

No, I say. You didn't.

He drives me to his house, on a small road that winds through evergreen trees. Occasionally, in the headlights, there is a glimpse of craggy landscape, reeds bent against a wind, and houses, white ones mostly, tucked within. Nothing is presented face-first as it would be in a suburban mainland town. It's too dark for me to tell what it really looks like here. I can only sense the stony body of the island, the aus-

terity of its dry grasses. And around us the immensity of water,
though the coastline disappears as we drive through the island's interior. I wonder why, of all possible places, the old painter has chosen to
live here in isolation. When I last knew him he was a gregarious, challenging, sociable man.

I am sitting in the passenger seat, my hands folded in my lap. My
nails have grown out while on tour and I need to trim them. I would
have noticed this earlier if I had been typing, if I had been writing,
which I haven't. Words are rising in my throat, and I can tell he wants
me to speak, to say something, but I examine each sentence as it arises
and not one feels right. *Why did you. Why are you. How did you find
me.* No. I am cold; I'm being cold to him. I don't have anything to say
yet.

There is some sound. The hum of the car, which is loud enough
that I can barely hear each of us breathing. The pounding of my heart,
which only I can hear.

I didn't think you'd come. I didn't think I would, either; maybe no
reasonable person would have come. Not after what had happened. I
had been so determined to leave all that in my past, to bury it under
the narrative I had created, and I had almost succeeded. But there was
another part of me, the part that is a writer, that wanted to know what
he was going to say. *A conversation*, he'd written. He had asked to
speak in person. Offered to pay for my flights and the ferry, as soon as
I wanted, as much as it cost, if I would come see him. And talk. And
so I came.

The old painter gestures with one hand toward the window. In
the darkness of the car I make out the ghostly reflection of his hand in
the glass. There's a grocery store down that road, he says, punctur-
ing the silence. And a restaurant. Those are the shops, those and the
area down by the ferry terminal. The rest of the island is houses. It's

mostly families here, dynasties. Most of the houses here have been passed down for generations.

There have been a few newcomers, he says. Like me.

I look out the window, where he's pointing, though we've already passed the turn, and trees are rushing past the window. I know that when I see this road again in daylight I won't recognize it. For some reason I can't look at the old painter directly. I don't want to know what is on his face, to see how it's changed. I'm worried that if I look at him, he'll look at me, and something will open, open before I'm ready. I'm nervous. I can feel my pulse in my throat. But threaded through that anxiety, wire-thin and just as bright, is something electric and alert, kindred to the feeling I used to feel around him, the feeling that I was on the verge of becoming.

I have the sense that something is being drawn between us. Not drawn as in line but as in arrow pulled back. But I don't know which one of us holds the bow, and which of us faces the arrow.

The old painter is restless. My stillness perturbs him. I wasn't like this when I was young. I'd been eager to please then, full of light and movement. One of his hands fiddles with a place on the steering wheel where the leather trim has peeled away. I can see his age in his hands, the thickness of his knuckles, the dryness of his fingertips. I have a sudden vision of the two of us encased in a silent bubble of air, moving through a tube of fluid. He speaks again.

How was your trip?

I'm a little tired, I say.

He doesn't say anything.

We take another turn and water comes into view again. Before it, a field. Along it a rocky beach, with a dock that extends far into the water. I take note of this. We turn again onto a gravel driveway where a house stands, its back to the sea. His house. All around us are these strange, grassy purple-flowered plants that I've never seen, illuminated by the car's headlights as if by a camera flash. Shadows loom.

He gets out of the car, opens the door for me. Goes to the trunk to retrieve my suitcase. There's a small landing, slate flagstones, where I wait. He unlocks the door, opens it. The lights are on inside.

Come in, he says. I want to show you my new paintings.

The old painter has been painting seascapes.

There is one on an easel, unfinished, in his living room. Four huge windows, each reaching nearly from floor to ceiling, look out onto the sea; a long wooden bench, lined with cushions, runs across the span of glass.

The seascape is small. He is working small here, smaller than he has ever worked. His finished canvases are stacked along the walls; some rest, faces up, on the wooden bench. In the painting on the easel the ocean is rough, choppy, the oils thickly laid. There's a horizon line, a streak of sky. Something amateurish about the scene. Still wet. But the colors are good, even under the flat indoor lights; he has always known what color a thing is. The room smells of turpentine.

He really is old, I see; I'm surprised at his aging, at the decade that seems to have collapsed in an instant. But I'm older now too, and this makes us peers. We are nearly the same height. I can't tell if it's because I hold myself taller now or if he's shrunk.

These are unlike you, I say.

When I knew him, and when he gained fame, he painted abstract scenes, with lines in caustic, perfect colors that cut through other shapes.

They are, he agrees. But I can't stop making them.

He is still handsome. Eyes a piercing gray. His hair is short, buzzed nearly to the skin at his temples. I can see the shape of his head more clearly now, and the way age has cut lines into his cheeks. He looks rugged here, like the Maine landscape has eroded away something of him. Thinner than he was. The whites of his eyes are yellowed, or maybe it's from the harsh lighting in the room.

There is something different about him. I can't place it. It's more than time passing, more than the accumulation of years.

He moved here full-time after retiring, he tells me.

When was that?

We are being formal with each other. Our voices cool. I am standing with my hands clasped in front of me. Still in my coat, though it is warm in the house. He has already turned on the heat, though it's only August. Then again, this feels the farthest north I've ever been.

Two years ago, he says.

And you live alone.

Yes.

He takes me on a tour: A big kitchen with a ceramic sink. High-backed wooden chairs ringing an oval dining table. He bought this house decades ago as a vacation home, he says. I'd never known about it. He'd begun to think about permanently moving here after having a minor stroke while he was still teaching. I'd never known about that, either. There's so much I don't know about him. He shows me the guest room, a twin bed with a window and a desk. And here's the bathroom you can use, he tells me. His room is at the end of the hall; he gestures toward it vaguely. Another bathroom, en suite, he says, now there's laundry here, he points, and here's the closet with clean linens, and here's another room that he used to use as a studio, but now he just paints outside. In the living room, you mean, I say, and he says yes that's what he meant.

The other room is packed with canvases and plastic bins stained with paint. There's a broken easel in the corner and a table, and a sawhorse with a glass palette across the top. I can't make out what the other paintings look like; they either lean together or are placed with their faces flush against the wall. Though there's a window in the room, the shade is pulled shut; it's darker than the rest of the house.

I want to know if he is thinking of what I am thinking of now, of the scene in the book where my character destroys his paintings, one by one, tearing them to shreds. His favorite part.

I pull my suitcase into the guest room.

Thank you, I say.

For it's true that I am a guest in his house.

When he walks away from me he moves quickly, sturdily, one hand thumping against the wall. As if to keep his balance. Another hand at his abdomen, holding himself lightly. That's new, too.

In the guest room there is a small closet that has plastic hangers on a rod below a wooden shelf and I put away my things, methodically, folding what can't be hung and placing it on the shelf. The room is nearly all window, with a desk I don't think I will ever write at. Still, I take out my laptop. A notebook. A pen. It is so dark here, the sky somehow liquid with it. When I press a hand to the window and cup it around my eyes to block the light from the overhead fixture, I can see tall waves of grass making undulating shapes in the wind. Beyond them, water. From the ferry ride I know it is a darker, deeper blue than the ocean I'm used to. Colder, too. I'm not sure how long I'll stay. I've already canceled the rest of my book tour. I couldn't imagine continuing to travel, to hold up my novel and read from it, not when he called me here.

It's hot in the room to the point of discomfort; it's small, and a heating vent is right beneath the window. I strip off my coat, my sweater. Hang those in the closet, too.

Without wanting to, exactly, I remember a night in college, before we'd ever had a meal together, before I'd ever been to a house of his.

It had been winter, and I was working late in the studio. It must have been my junior year; I had just enrolled in his course for the spring semester. Though it was January, the department building was overheated, stuffily hot, and I had developed a method of layering my painting clothes—tiny, ill-fitting gym shorts that rode up my ass, paired with an oversize T-shirt—under sweatshirt, scarf, and puffer coat to make the walk to the studios, stripping down as soon as I was inside again.

It was late to be in a university building, or maybe that was just how it felt then, the night flat against the windowpanes. The utter bleakness of those winter nights surprised me when I first moved East, the sky moving straight from gray to black on overcast days, no blue in between. I was crouched over a canvas—at that age, I often liked to work on the floor—and in my memory, I'm wearing running shoes, and my hair is filthy. I remember that the room smelled like mineral spirits, and it also smelled like me.

When the door opened, I was startled; I stood up quickly, dropping my brush. It left a mark on the canvas and then rolled across the floor.

Sorry, the old painter said. He knelt to pick it up and gave it back to me.

I've ruined your painting, he said.

You didn't, I said.

When I dropped to my knees again to wipe away the mark, he stopped me. Wait, he said. Put it on the wall. I don't understand why you young people never use easels.

Because they're heavy and unwieldy and make me feel like I want to die, I didn't tell him. Instead, I hung the painting on the two thumb-tacks that usually held it flush against the studio wall. Together we stepped back to look at it.

Before I arrived at the fast, fluid form of the studies, I had been making paintings of landscapes, drawn from blurry photographs I took on moving cars and trains. The paintings were fine, neither good nor bad, efforts toward something I was still trying to understand. Though I longed to make work with the fine-grained minutiae of Frances's, I wasn't that kind of painter, and I wanted to learn what kind of painter I was.

The falling brush had left an uneven dark-green smear in a blue-gray patch of sky. I would wipe it away, I remembered thinking even then, and I knew the old painter agreed that it added nothing. But he pointed to a different part of the canvas, a place where the image broke apart into abstraction.

Is this wet or dry? he asked, a finger hovering.

It's still wet, I said.

This part, he said, drawing a circle with his index finger. This is interesting, here. What the color is doing.

We looked at it together. You're making it something other than what it was, he said. That's good.

Then he stiffened, as though he had only just realized the lateness of the hour and had somewhere else to be. Or maybe it was my body he was noticing, my bare legs, the smell of me in the overheated room.

He stepped away from me then.

Good night, he said.

Good night.

I wiped the mark from the canvas that night, and cleaned the jagged streak of paint left on the floor. When I picked up my brush again to use it, I had to rinse it, too; dirt and dust had become embedded in the bristles, and despite some difficulty, I managed to make it clean and workable again.

It's only now, years later, that I'm able to imagine myself in any position except for the one that I had taken. I wonder what he had been thinking when he stepped into the studio that late. Or what the interaction had led him to think. For a moment, I feel as though we're all four of us—as we were then, as we are now—in this house. This house where I am staying, with no return flight, no exit plan.

This ought to scare me. But that quick, alive part of me, the part that has teeth, feels excited by it. Bites down.

A knock at the door—the door is open; he's knocked on the wall next to it. I've been looking out the window, though with the light on, all I can see is my reflection, golden against the glass. It's late, or it feels late. Everything feels flat because of the blackness of the windows. I've been traveling since the early morning, and even in the dim reflection, I can see dark circles under my eyes.

There's dinner, the old painter says. On the table. I'm going to bed. He pauses. If you don't mind.

It's fine, I say.

Right, he says. He closes his eyes, briefly, as if in pain. When he opens them again he's not looking directly at me. We have so much to say to each other, but I don't know how to say it, or where to begin.

Go to sleep, I say. I'll be fine.

Dinner is a sandwich from a stand by the ferry terminal. It's wrapped in wax paper; he's put the package, still taped together, on a plate. Upon taking my first bite I realize I haven't eaten since my lay-over in Dallas, and I eat quickly, voraciously even, pausing only to wipe smears of mayonnaise and crumbs from my face. I wash the plate in the sink and place it on the drying rack, then search for a trash can. I open cupboards, feeling like I'm intruding. I'm curious about the old painter, about how he lives. Why he is here. Why he's asked me to come. I want to linger, to investigate, to open more drawers and doors. But instead I find the trash can, in the place where I thought it would be, shove the paper wrapping inside, and shut the lid.

———

There's a bit of moonlight that makes its way into my room. With the overhead lights off I can almost see by it. It's been a long, disorienting day and I can't sleep.

I get out of bed and change my clothes without turning on the lights, judging by shape and silhouette: sweatpants, a long-sleeved shirt. The hardwood floors are cold beneath my bare feet. In the en-tryway of the house I put on my sneakers without bothering with socks. When I look down the hallway to the old painter's room, there's no light beneath the door. He must be asleep. The front door is unlocked, and after I slip out I silently press it shut, feeling the latch click.

The dock isn't far, down a winding mown path that skirts the edge of the water. Tall grasses sweep at my legs and leave lines of wet dew. I reach the entrance and open the gate, stepping onto the wooden dock, which is slippery with moss and algae. It's hard to see, though my eyes have adjusted, and I move carefully. The dock extends over the water, over the waves of seaweed growing in the shallows, sloping down to meet the sea's surface, where three floating panels are lashed together, striped buoys bobbing in the water nearby. There are two boats moored here, one with a motor, the other a tiny rowboat. They must have names, painted somewhere on their sides, but I can't see them.

I walk down the dock, down to the water. I can smell the ocean, and hear it, a low rushing. The shapes of the other islands are massed and dark at the horizon, and in the cloudless sky I see a sliver of white moon.

A breeze moves the reeds on either side of me, a whisper coming through the grass. There is something particular about the quality of this night, and though it's colder here than it is there, the air reminds me of nights I've spent in Asia, by the seaside, where the wind blew through my clothes at such a perfect level of humidity that it felt as though I was completely naked, with nothing between me and the air.

The ocean is calm. Tiny waves lap against the floating dock. I take off my shoes. Then I strip off my clothes, leaving everything in a neat pile. If I disappeared tonight, it would be my evidence, that I had come here. To do what, I'm not sure. I put both hands on the metal railing of the ladder that descends into the sea, and then, before I can be afraid, I drop into the water.

It's colder than I expect. My body comes achingly alive in it. I inhale huge gulps of air, my first deep breaths in months; the feeling is sharp and sweet in my lungs. How had I forgotten about this? All of my blood has come to the surface of my body; I feel a grimace stretching my cheeks. I dip my head beneath the waves, rise up to blink away the salt. Then blink faster, harder. When the salt water runs into my mouth I taste it. My face wet. Night sky enormous and full of stars.

And when I look down I see there are stars, too, in the water. Tiny pricks of light, splashes of illumination that slip off my bare arms and back into the sea. When I move my hands around they send up small, glittering flashes, and I do this, watching. Then I raise one hand and particles of light stream down my palm in streaks. I have never seen bioluminescence like this. I had not known it could be found here. When I disturb the water and see the sparks, I almost feel happy. Something close to it. Solid, bright.

Once, when I was a child, my parents and I took a road trip down the coast to visit family. We stopped in a seaside town that had a boardwalk and a pier. This was early in the trip, and I was still excited to see these small towns, to walk on the boardwalk and buy saltwater taffy, though I didn't particularly like it then and as an adult I almost never buy sweets. It was the colors I enjoyed, the different flavors, so various, and the names they were called; I liked to see the taffy being pulled on a machine, and then neatly cut and wrapped. It was outside the shop that I saw the woman seated on a wrought-iron bench on the boardwalk.

I didn't know her story then, I will never know it, but even then I remember thinking she was strange; she was my mother's age, maybe older, and she was dressed in many layers of clothing that looked hand-sewn, with bright colors and pleats. She looked as though she might be an artist, a woman who made things to sell to tourists, and she was crying, something had distressed her, but the cries she let out were unlike any cry I had heard before. They were sonorous, guttural, they seemed to be wrenched out of her body, wordless, and they went on. She was not embarrassed, she did not bend her body over as she wept. My mother, seeing her, hearing her, put her hand over my ear, her fingers cupping my face, and we turned and walked away.

I think of that woman now, or maybe it's the sound of my own actions that recalls her to me, as I open my mouth and let out a shout, a strange call, it's something between *ha* and *oh*, a noise that doesn't sound like a human made it but more like the sound of something falling, clanging against the sides of an immense and deep well. It's a sound I have never heard myself make. *Ha*, I say, *oh*, *O*, shouting into the dark. *O*. I imagine the sound of my voice carrying across the flat surface of the ocean.

If I am crying I do not know it. All around me is salt, and wet, and sea.

When I return to the house, carrying my shoes in one hand, dripping water onto the hardwood floors, everything is silent, every light off. The old painter won't know that I ever left. I take a shower, turning the temperature as high as it will go, and it must be the hot water after the cold shock of the ocean that finally tranquilizes me, and in the guest room I sink into a deep and dreamless sleep.

=

The old painter is already in the living room when I wake. He has made coffee, and without asking I help myself to some from the pot, still warm. It's early, just past seven. The sunlight woke me; my room has thin curtains, which I didn't pull shut.

My room. I shouldn't put it that way.

There's an eclectic collection of mugs in the kitchen, none of them matching. For some reason it is this detail that humanizes him to me. There are mugs from national parks, museums, conferences. All things he experienced before he entered my life, and I his. I take down a mug, it's from the Art Institute of Chicago. It has a painting printed on it, one of Monet's haystacks, though the transfer has faded and rubbed away in places.

I went here on my book tour, I say. The Art Institute, I add, because I realize the old painter isn't facing me and can't see what I am holding.

You gave a talk there? he asks.

No, I say. I don't know how to explain it, how I got there, the mix-up with my suitcase. I met someone there, I say.

Hmm, he says.

The old painter is sitting in a chair that looks out onto the sea, his easel at his shoulder. He doesn't seem to have been working. For some reason I can't bear to enter the living room, not fully; it feels too much like his domain, and I stand in the doorway of the kitchen instead. In daylight, the four windows of the living room are resplendent with landscape, all gray sky and air and flat sea. It stuns me. I think of the word *promontory*. Then I wonder where I learned it.

Christine, he says. I try to keep my shoulders from reacting. It's still so strange to hear him say my name. How'd you sleep?

Fine, I answer.

Come here, he says.

I take a sip of the coffee but don't move.

Are you scared of me?

No, I say.

Then come. There's something I want you to see.

He's risen from his chair and I step into the room. I go to the window, where he is pointing at a shape on the horizon. It's cloudy today, still no rain. I can only just make out a tower, white against the trees. It sits on a rocky island, bare except for the tall, lonely structure.

It's a lighthouse, I say.

Defunct now, he answers, it fell out of use in the fifties. Too hard to convince any lighthouse keeper to live there. I spent a night in it alone as a boy.

You grew up here?

My grandparents had a house. Not this one. But a house out here. I spent summers here when I was young. I didn't get along with my father, so it was boarding school during the year, and summers they sent me out here.

I try to remember where he grew up. Boston, I think, something like that. The suburbs. Boarding school, so he must have been wealthy.

We used to try to swim out to the lighthouse, he says. At the beginning of the season it always seemed so attainable. But once in the water it was much farther than we thought, nearly a mile. And of course there was the matter of swimming back to shore once you had gotten to the island.

Other times, he says, the times we actually went out there, we'd take the boat out. Not a skiff like the one I have now, a rowboat. During the day you could climb up into the lighthouse and see where the huge lantern once was. There was broken glass on the floor and you had to walk carefully. You could see miles from there on a clear day. It was enough to make you feel like you were king of the world.

I don't say anything. I wonder who this *we* is, picture a fleet of young, privileged boy-men. Cousins, maybe, or neighbors, classmates.

They dared me to do it, he says now. Spend a night up there. I was the youngest and smallest, and as a result had the most to prove, so of course I agreed.

I think they were just trying to give me a scare, he says. We had been there during the day, plenty of times, we knew there was nothing frightening. Living, maybe, there were creatures, animals, but not frightening, it wasn't as though it was haunted by the ghost of an old lighthouse keeper—that's what you thought I was going to say, wasn't it? That there was a ghost?

No, I say.

Hmm, he says again.

We knew it wasn't haunted, he continues. So I say yes, we decide I'll go that weekend, and I start planning, it's only a few days away. I'm deciding what to bring, a flashlight, provisions, gear, water, I even pack a little dinner for myself—

How old were you?

Oh, he says, twelve, maybe thirteen.

Go on, I say.

I'm looking out the window, my eyes fixed on the lighthouse. It looks tiny, innocuous at this distance, like a model you'd place in a train set.

So we decide we'll go to the lighthouse in two boats, he says. The other boys will drop me off and leave one rowboat for me to get back. So I can run back home if I get scared, they say. They're already teasing me, laughing. But it's a calm night and I'm not afraid. I tell them to just tie it up for me, but they'll see, they'll come back in the morning and I'll be there, happy as a clam, maybe I'll even be making pancakes.

The journey out is fine, he says. We leave in the afternoon. They're hassling me for bringing so much stuff. I've brought a sleeping bag, extra clothes, a gallon of water, a plastic cooler of food. What I've forgotten to bring is matches, but I don't know that yet, I'm on the boat and we're rowing out and one of the kinder boys is rowing for me, to do me a favor, as I'm the one who has to spend the night alone in the lighthouse.

So we get there and then the first thing goes wrong. As I'm unloading my things someone drops my spare clothes in the water. It's fine, I tell him, it's an honest mistake, I'll hang them to dry—I shouldn't have said that, the boys immediately start teasing me again, they say, Oh, what a *lady*, what a *girlie-girl*, he's going to hang his *laundry* in the lighthouse—and I'm upset and I don't want to act like I care, so I leave my clothes out on the rocks. That's the second thing. By the time all my things are unloaded everyone else is restless and they want dinner. So they leave. They take the second boat as planned and I'm alone on the island.

For the first few hours I'm as happy as can be. I look down to where I can see my rowboat and it pleases me. I make a little shelter for myself in the top of the lighthouse and arrange all my gear. I eat the dinner I packed for myself. Eventually the sun goes down, and it begins to get cold. No problem, I think, I've got my sleeping bag. So I get inside and I think it'll be fine to wait things out.

I've fallen asleep, and it can't be that late when it happens, but it's so dark that it feels like midnight. I hear this whooping, this hollering, and a bunch of bandits dressed in black, their faces painted, have stormed up the tower.

Of course, the old painter says, it was just the same boys, dressed up to terrify me, wearing masks, with coal smeared all over their faces. But at the time they were unrecognizable, they looked purely demonic. They made a mess of my campsite and then they held me down and stripped off all my clothes to humiliate me.

I'm sorry, I say.

It couldn't have lasted more than five minutes, the old painter says. They flung everything around and then they left.

I'm sorry, I say again.

He sits down now, his gaze still on the horizon. Settles back into his chair.

A storm blew in later that night, he says. It rained all night, coming in through the windows. I didn't have anything to make a fire. Not that making a fire up there would have been a good idea at all, but I was desperate, and cold, and wet, and miserable. I'd even cut my arm on the broken glass and had nothing to patch it up. The storm went on into the next morning, and it was too dangerous to row back out again, though I thought about it. I'd have been stranded there another night if it weren't for one of their fathers, who came out in a boat to get me. When he picked me up I was already sick. I had a fever, I was practically half drowned. I stayed in bed for weeks after that, recovering, and then it was time to go back to school.

What happened to the other boys? I ask. I don't know what I'm expecting him to say.

Nothing, he answers. They were worried sick when they realized that I was stuck out there, but it was for their skins, not mine. They hadn't told anyone that I was there, not until morning. When I was sick, they visited, but I knew only some of them were sorry. My father, though. When he found out what happened, he was the angriest I'd ever seen him. He thought I was an idiot for agreeing to go, and an even bigger idiot for not being prepared for the storm. He really gave me a thrashing.

The old painter is silent for a moment.

Then I went off to school, he says, and we didn't speak again for almost five years, when I told him that I was going to study painting in college. He wasn't happy about that, either.

We're quiet. Together and not together, me standing, him sitting, both of us looking out the window. I can feel him resurfacing, coming back through the years.

And you can see it from here, I say.

The old painter shrugs. You can see that lighthouse from most anywhere on this shore.

I wonder if it haunts him, if he's bought this house to keep it in sight, if he's in fact afraid of forgetting how it felt. It's strange how we do that. How we think: This wound feels like home, I will make my home in this wound. But I had done that; I had believed that this wound was all I knew.

Aloud I say, That's not your tragic backstory.

I don't know why I'm being so cruel.

No, he says. No. He half coughs, half makes a noise in his throat. Just a horrible thing that happened to a horrible man long ago.

I turn to him, take in the sight of him in his chair. His aged, handsome face. His one hand resting on his heart, as though feeling for something. As I watch him he moves it to his abdomen, then back up to his heart.

You're not horrible, I say.

Sure, he says. Sure.

I can feel him turning away from me, and in response, I turn away from him. A bird cuts across the sky. I watch it pass through one, two, three, four windows before it flies out of sight. Its body is the shape a pen makes when you drop it on paper. Its path the line.

In the kitchen he rattles around, making breakfast. Is there anything you don't eat, he asks me. No, I say, there isn't. Though he already knows this. When he used to have me over to his house in B——, he always cooked for us. He'd pour me a glass of wine and I'd sit at the counter, drinking slowly, watching him with appreciation. He was always unwrapping things I'd never tried and setting them before me: expensive cheeses; tinned fish in oil; once, a block of foie gras, velvet and pink.

When I first started at the MFA program, before we grew close, I'd gone to a party he hosted at the beginning of the school year. He was charming, expansive in his hospitality—a sociable man, that's how I remember him; he greeted everyone with familiarity and by name. His home was beautiful, a stately Victorian, furnished by generations of academics past, and I remember arriving a little too early, wandering through the high-ceilinged rooms, touching surfaces, once even passing my hand through the flame of a candle just to see how it felt, until the rooms filled with people and the party overflowed onto the street. That September he often hosted our graduate cohort for dinner—to get to know us better, he said, though in his voice it sounded like a challenge, and we'd fall over ourselves trying to impress him with what we were reading and what we had seen. Each time, I'd leave drunk, flushed with pleasure, delighted to be invited in.

Later, when our dinners became just the two of us, we'd talk endlessly about painting, red wine sloshing in the bowls of our glasses. He'd put forth an argument, advance as I parried. I was exhilarated by the world he presented: an arena where art was champion, where there was nothing more important, more worthy, than the act of making. By the time of the second party he held, just after midterm, I'd grown at ease with him. Comfortable enough to stay at the end of the evening to help tidy up, watching as my classmates shrugged on their coats and disappeared onto the darkened streets.

Near the end of the semester, I was at his house at least one evening a week, and he began to teach me how to cook. Even as a graduate student, I had almost zero kitchen skills; an only child raised by doting, anxious parents, I ate my mother's home-cooked meals every day of my childhood, and whenever I became curious or, more often, bored of my books, I was shooed out of the kitchen and encouraged to study. In college, I had subsisted on dining-hall swipes and sandwiches that I split with Frances. The first time the old painter asked me to dice an onion, I didn't know how to prepare it, that I should keep the root intact, trimming only the top to pull back the papery skins. When I began slicing into the onion, using a knife entirely the wrong size, I'd sent a chunk of it flying across the countertop, and the old painter had descended then, taking knife and onion out of my hands.

Hold the knife like this, he said, taking a chef's knife and pinching it between forefinger and thumb. Let the weight of the blade slice through. There. He sliced the onion in half, then sliced again, making vertical cuts, avoiding the root. Like that, he said. He handed me the knife. Try it, he said.

I followed as he instructed. Felt the shift in my hand, the material weight, the way the tool was perfect for the task. A knife was no different from a brush: Each was beholden to the mark it made.

Then slice across, he said, watching me work. Then horizontally, he said. Yes. Like that.

I finished chopping. Lifted my hands and wiped the last fine pieces clinging to the blade.

Good, he had said, surveying my work, looking pleased.

The old painter is making omelets now, beating eggs in a bowl. He flicks water onto the pan, a cast-iron. It's a pan I recognize, and this moves me. I could soften toward him, I think. It's been ten years. There's a smell of butter in the air, sautéed onions. He sets a steaming plate on the table, at the place that I've gathered is his, then another one for me.

Go on, he says, nodding.

I want to know why he's asked me here.

I sit down with him, align my back with the high-backed chair, and together we eat.

So tell me about your work now, he says.

We've finished breakfast and he has leaned back, lazily, his eyes appraising me. I am sitting upright, my elbows close to my torso, while he is spread out. I imagine his legs, loose beneath the table. I recognize this posture of his, his look of satisfaction, and brace myself.

What do you mean, I say.

Tell me about what you're working on.

You mean the book?

No, he says, I mean, are you *working* on anything.

The book, I say again, uncomprehending. That's what I've been working on. For the last few years.

No, he says again, that's not work, I mean to ask are you making anything, are you painting?

I stare at him. That was my work, I say.

But you must still be painting, he says.

I'm not painting anymore.

I see, he says.

I bite down, hard, on the inside of my lower lip. Make a fist of my left hand, nails digging into my palm, then release it slowly. There are little crescents where my nails have pressed; I watch as they fill in with color.

Why not? he asks.

I blink, hard. My mind goes white. You know why, I say, and I rise and leave the room. It takes every cell in my body not to slam the door.

In the guest room, I pack again, roughly, tossing clothes into my suitcase without folding them. I shouldn't have come. I shouldn't have thought he had anything to say to me. I should have known he wanted to humiliate me one more time, that he thought nothing of it, the same way he thought nothing of me. I'm crying, hard, bitter tears that, when I slip my tongue out to catch them, sting the cracks in my lips. I taste blood.

Christine, he calls. I hear his voice as though from very far away. Christine, he says again, his voice closer, Christine, he says, now nearly shouting.

I'm on the floor, on my knees, my back straight, my body aflame.

Why did you ask me to come here, I say.

Christine, he says once more.

Yes, I say. I lift my head to look at him.

He is standing above me. His face is strange in this light—his skin gone yellow and gray. He puts a hand to the place just below his sternum. Exhales slowly.

I'm dying, he says.

He'd noticed it at the start of spring. Pain in his back and abdomen, trouble digesting. He'd been losing weight and had issues with his stomach that were amorphous and confusing. After the stroke, after he retired and moved out to Maine, he'd thought he would have more time. He was healthy, he thought; he had recovered well; he swam every day.

He was in a bookstore on the mainland when he saw my name on the cover of a novel. He was living there at the time; he had rented a room near the hospital, where he was going through tests of every kind, hoping to learn what was wrong with him. He had walked into the store hoping to find something to read to pass the time between doctors' appointments. He was pleased to see my book; he had wondered what became of me after I left the program, and he bought it and began reading it that evening.

Meanwhile. He was still undergoing exams. He was getting his blood drawn, vials and vials of it; he had an endoscopy, a colonoscopy; he had CAT scans and ultrasounds. In each the intrusion was worse than the pain itself, which at first was merely baffling, without cause. In between tests, when he had the energy, he read my book. He carried it around with him; it almost became a kind of talisman. He'd read it in the waiting room, a paragraph here, a page there, and what he realized, as he went from room to room in the hospital, his veins inflamed, his stomach bloated and filled with dye and drained again, was that the book was a grotesque kind of mirror. He couldn't put it down; he kept reading, transfixed by how it seemed to be exactly as things had passed between us, and at the same time nothing like what had really happened. Events had been stretched and distorted, almost beyond recognition, but there remained a grain of truth, one that caught in his eye and stung. And as he read on, in waiting rooms, on hospital beds, it seemed I had really meant it, everything I said, that what was in the text was what I believed, or worse, was what I felt. It was like being probed from the inside out, no, a vivisection, to see our relationship like that on the page, everything revealed, everything bared. When he finished it, alone in his rented room, he wept.

After waiting for the final tests to be reviewed, he was diagnosed with late-stage pancreatic cancer. Though at first his doctors urged him to consider it, because he was in fact still relatively young, he was not interested in radiation, in chemotherapy, in prolonging his life in a painful or uncomfortable way. He lived alone; he was unmarried; he was estranged from his surviving family. He would take pain meds, he decided, he would take the palliative route, ride it out until he couldn't anymore, and when he died no one would be sorry.

When I left for Maine I disappeared from the social world, the old painter says. That world that you and I knew.

I am still on the floor. Legs tucked beneath me, hands resting on my knees. He has come to sit on the bed, one hand fisted in the covers. He's too close, but I don't move away. I cannot tear my eyes from him. His mouth is dry; I see the cracking at the corners of his lips. My mouth is dry, too.

How quickly an old man disappears, he says. No one has called on me. No one is wondering about me. I had fantasized about disappearing, about dying in solitude. Another white man bites the dust. But then I remembered your book.

It was perversely comforting, he says.

My stomach twists.

As damning as it was, he continues. As shocking as it was. I was dying, I had already died one kind of death, and I was comforted to know that someone was thinking about me. So I looked you up. I found your work. I saw you were successful and that you were traveling. And then yes, I wrote to you. I wanted you to know I was there. Listening. I wanted you to know I was real, that I could speak. I thought nothing would come of it, that it would be the last act of a dying man.

He laughs, suddenly; it's short, with the quality of a bark.

But then you wrote back.

Yes, I say.

I had.

You are the only person I want to speak to, he says. Now that I know I'm dying.

I take a deep breath, exhale through my nose. My eyes are stinging. After all this time, I feel it again, hate myself for feeling it, even in this new and charged form. That high, piercing sweetness. The pleasure of being chosen.

I'm sorry, I say. Though that's not what I mean to say.

He inclines his faded head.

Will you stay for a while, he says. Not long. Just to spend a little time.

I look at him. A bolt of pain forms, softens in my throat.

I'll stay, I answer.

MAINE

≡

Now that I know he's dying, I see the signs of illness everywhere in his house. I don't know how I managed to miss them. I was too busy looking for something else. They remain: The stack of laboratory reports and bills, still sealed in their envelopes on the kitchen counter. The pain pills in plastic orange bottles that are sent rattling when I open a drawer, looking for a pair of scissors that I never find. The jaundiced color of his skin. Though he is clearly sick, he insists he is well enough to go for his daily swim. To the buoy and back, he says. The buoy is maybe one-third of the distance between here and the lighthouse. From the living room I watch him swim until I can no longer see him, and then, against all expectations, he comes back. Each morning he returns from the water as I am pouring my second cup of coffee.

Sometimes when he returns we speak to each other. Sometimes I don't want to talk to him and I go for long walks alone, pushing the tall reeds aside with one hand. The world, which I once thought was so expansive and full of potential, has narrowed to this fine, luminous point, this island and the coast on which this house is built. But from here I can see everything.

A promontory is a feature, often geological but sometimes man-made, where a high point of land juts out over the sea.

I know this now because I looked it up in the dictionary in the old painter's library.

When he sees me standing over the dictionary, he says, You can write here, you know. He has seen my laptop and my notebooks, still shut like clamshells, laid out on the little desk in the guest room.

But something about the way he says it hurts me and I turn away, act like I was merely flipping through pages, like I wasn't looking for anything.

Still. It is easier than I thought, staying here with him. It's not pity I feel, seeing him aged and sick and weakened, though I don't know what it is I feel if it's not that. I can't tell if I hate him now or if I don't. Sometimes I'm certain I still do.

I can't admit this to him, I know he'd be too pleased to hear it, but it's also the beauty of the landscape that keeps me here, mesmerized. The austere silhouette of stone against sea. The sight of the ocean and the immense quiet of the island seem to nourish some unseen part of me. I had never known I wanted this. In the evenings, after the old painter has retired for the night, I go swimming, to see the biolumi-nescence. But that remains my secret.

One morning, walking, I discover a forest of kelp, waving beneath the water. The air is so cold and clear, and the movement of the

seaweed so beautiful, that I stand there for several minutes, just looking.

There's something I still want to ask him. I'll know when.

=

Not long after I decide to stay at his house, I trim my nails in the bathroom. There's something weird and intimate about it, like shitting in
his house, which I've also already done. I sit on the edge of the bath-
tub and my nail clippings land in the trash. I wonder if he can hear me,
if he recognizes the click, click. After, my hands look soft, denuded; I
miss the claws they became. I've cut some of my nails too short, and
they feel tender. There's a little redness, where I've trimmed too close
to the quick.

=

What did you see in Chicago?

What?

What show, he says, impatiently.

Oh.

It's afternoon. The afternoons here are slow. Every day is slow
and filled with white light. I haven't been here long—two days, three,
but I'm already forgetting what my life was like before I arrived. The
old painter is seated at his easel. I have been reading, a book I found
in his library.

Nothing too interesting, I say. Sixties paintings. Ab Ex, mostly.

The usual, then, he says. I know he wishes he had been one of
them, a Pollock or a Motherwell, a cowboy formalist flinging his seed

into eternity. But he was only a boy in the sixties, and to me those men are art history.

Though there was a Vija Celmins, I say. In the show. I was surprised.

Who's that? he asks.

You don't know Celmins?

No, he says. Should I?

Probably, I say. Though I'm not surprised he doesn't know.

I step down into the living room to show him a picture of the Celmins seascape on my phone, increasing the size and brightness so he can see it. But even as I do this I know it's a failed endeavor, he can't possibly make out what's so special about the painting, and after a moment he makes a noise that indicates he'd agree.

It's done in oils, I say. Not dissimilar from the work the old painter himself is making. But where his seascapes have a rough, choppy look, Celmins's painting is nearly photographic in its realism. Beautiful as I'd found the painting when I saw it, the small screen of my phone has killed its magic, and I can see he's not impressed. He lifts his head, he's a little like a dog in this way, in the physical, weary way he communicates now, and together we look out onto the actual sea. It's a string of cloudy days we've had, and I know he wants it to clear up so he can go out on his boat.

I've always liked Celmins, I say.

Hmm.

I like her terrifying realism. Her total subjection to the pure power of the image.

Hmm, he says again. I can tell he's thinking about something else.

Frances is still painting, I say.

That gets his attention, and he turns to me.

Frances Song, I say. We were classmates. I saw her in L.A.

Sure, I remember her. Shy little Frances. I used to see the two of you together all the time. One small, one tall.

She wasn't shy so much as she was quiet, I say.

I'm not sure why I'm defending her.

Great technical painter, he says. Though her work was always a little dull, wasn't it?

That's what everyone else in school said.

Oh? And what did you think of it, Christine?

Hearing my name coming from his mouth jars me, makes me wonder why I'm broaching any of this.

I thought it was good, I say. Inwardly I chide myself for sounding like a kid. *Good*. Was there no other word I could have used? I appreciated her consistency, I continue. She kept doing what she was doing, even when the feedback wasn't particularly good.

There it is again, that word *good*, the least interesting thing you can say about art or an artist, landing like a stone. Even though I have no intention of learning from him, I feel like a student again in front of the old painter, seeking his approval, trying to win him over with my way with words.

She's showing now?

In Los Angeles, yes. She's represented by a gallery there. And she's been in shows in New York. Fairs too, probably, I say, trying to keep the envy out of my voice.

Mm. And what do you think of that? he asks.

Something about his tone makes me look over at him. He's not disinterested, I see now, but watching me with a clear and canny eye.

The work is strong, I say. That's true, I believe that. She has an immediately recognizable style, I say aloud, and all of her work is in conversation with itself. But—

I think about what to say.

But I don't think the work is changing. Aside from some technical changes, and some shifts in style, her work really doesn't look that different from what she painted in school. I don't know if she's challenging herself enough, I say.

There, I think. That seems fair.

You think she's had it too easy, the old painter says.

No—well, painting *is* easy for her, I say. I hate the whine my voice pitches into and try to tone it down. Frances has that technical skill I always wanted, I say. It comes easily to her, I've seen her working. But I don't think she's pushing herself.

So you think being a great artist means pushing yourself, the old painter says.

Not necessarily, I say.

Then what is it?

I don't know, I say, suddenly angry with him. Storming out of the room would only make me feel like more of a child than I already do, so I stay.

I'm not an artist anymore, I say. I don't think about these things.

For a moment, I think I've surprised him enough to shut him up. He turns back to his canvas. He's working wet-in-wet, and there's a section of the sky painted extremely loose, almost puddling, the oils thinned down with turpentine. Roiling yellows and purples streak down into slate green, pigment gathering at the base of each mark. With his brush, he picks up a bit of dark-gray paint and dabs it into the sky. Thunderous clouds above a stormy sea. Though outside, the ocean is flat, the sky calm. The thinned paint trickles into the grooves the thicker brushstrokes have left. Watching him work, seeing his obvious pleasure in the medium, his comfort with letting the paint mingle and spread, I feel a surge of desire to return to it so strong my mouth hurts.

Then why did you paint? he asks me.

What?

You could have done any other kind of thing. Why painting?

For a moment, I don't answer.

I think Frances's paintings now are too commercial, I say instead. I know I'm being mean. But it's also what I think. She only cares about what sells, I say. That's why she isn't pushing herself.

She's successful, isn't she? the old painter says. Do you think she needs to suffer more?

No, I say. No. I know she suffers already.

I think about Frances, alone in her apartment, food rotting in the sink, ignoring my calls at the door. No. She suffers a lot.

The old painter makes a few more movements on the canvas. Light, glancing gestures, barely touching the surface.

I'm overworking this, he says.

Then stop.

As you wish, he says. He sets down his brush.

A year or two after I'd stopped painting, when I lived in the city and was dating Colin, I had a series of dreams about it. They were plotless, uncomplicated dreams, dreams in which I was painting, in which my hands moved with perfect ease. The gradual attunement of my body to a favorite brush; the buttery, heavy body of oil paint spread under the palette knife; the pleasure of one steady, graceful stroke: It was in those dreams that I returned most completely to what I had loved about painting, which was the medium itself, its own language beyond language. I loved that dance, so tactile, and I loved how wholeheartedly I dropped into it, the sweetness it gave me as sweet as any fruit.

I had once before posed for Frances, but she had also sat for me. I'd almost thought she wouldn't. It took asking her offhand, as we walked back to the studio one afternoon. I asked her like I was asking for a glass of water. Would you sit for me when we get back. She took a tiny sip of her coffee and I saw a feline sliver of her pink tongue. Okay, she said.

In the painting I made of Frances, she's sitting in front of her studio wall. She's wearing a white T-shirt, and, in my memory, black volleyball shorts. The canvas is closely cropped, and only her face and shoulders are in the frame. I'd liked the contrast of the values— her dark hair, her light shirt. I painted her face thinly, the background thick and wet. By then she'd switched to wearing contacts; with her hair pulled back, her face was open, beautiful and clear. I had tried hard at that, to capture what I found so compelling about her. Her hair and shoulders I blocked in first. Then the interior details: her mouth, nose. I worked lightly—whispers on the canvas, subtle shadows, almost watery. She spent most of the session looking down, her eyelids fluttering, the way they do when you're dreaming. In the very last minutes I asked her to look at me.

When I woke from my painting dreams, I always felt incredibly happy, and then incredibly sad. I never told Colin about the dreams— there were so many things I didn't tell him—and eventually, when I began writing more, and more seriously, they stopped.

Do you think you'll ever show these paintings? I ask the old painter. He has made at least one a day since I've arrived, sometimes two.

Maybe posthumously, he says.

Do you want me to organize a show?

Would you do that for me?

I think about it.

Probably not, I say.

With my eyes I track the movement of a shape on the horizon. A boat, maybe; it's big enough to be the ferry, though it's not the right time for it. I can't tell.

Do you think you were a great artist?

No, the old painter says.

Did you want to be?

Of course I did, he says. Doesn't everyone?

I didn't, I say.

Until I met Frances, I had always thought that artists were other people. Or was it that other people, people unlike me, were the people who became artists? No—I wanted to be an artist, but I didn't know how it happened. It seemed to be through some mysterious process that one was anointed. It was in the common room of Frances's dorm, drawing together on the floor, watching her work with such fierce intensity, that I understood that being an artist wasn't something that happened to you; it was something you did, something you decided for yourself. Even so, even after our late nights in the studio, even after I'd given hours and days of my life to painting, I had not thought it would be my life. And—perhaps I turned out to be right about that.

Did you put me up for that award? I ask him.

You won an award?

I want to smack him.

Yes. Senior year. The one for a female artist in the graduating class of H——. With the big check.

Oh, that. You won that?

Don't humiliate me, I say.

It was so long ago, Christine. It must have been—ten years ago, wasn't it?

When I won that prize, I say, Frances stopped speaking to me.

And. I keep my eyes fixed on the landscape now, not looking at him as I speak. After everything that happened, I wondered if you'd put me up for it, even though I didn't deserve it.

The old painter sighs. He's thinking about it now. I know, even if he tries to act like he doesn't remember, that he hasn't forgotten. Because he hasn't forgotten me.

Maybe it didn't matter to you then, I say. It doesn't matter now. But at the time, when I was young, it changed my life.

You're still young, he says.

It gave me hope, I say. And what I keep thinking about, I say, surprising myself that I'm even brave enough to say it. What I keep thinking about, what I keep asking myself is if that was a false hope. If I was actually any good or if it was just that you found me attractive, and you wanted something from me.

When I look at him I see that he looks pained. I'm not upset by this; there's a part of me that is glad to see that I can wound him.

Christine, he says.

Yes, I say.

Christine, he says again, I am sorry to make you my caretaker. But. There is a bottle of pills. In the kitchen drawer. The label says hydrocodone. Will you get them for me?

He is in real pain. Since I've arrived he has not asked me to do any of this, any of this medical caretaking. He has handled his own blood, his vomit, his medication. For a moment, I really want to make him suffer. I could ignore his request for pain pills. I could leave his house and walk into the sea. And though I do want to punish him, I do not want to punish him for relinquishing the control of his pain to me, and so I walk to the kitchen, retrieve the pill bottle, and return with a glass of water.

After he swallows, the old painter looks at me.

I did see something special in you, he says.

And then you killed it, I say.

An expression moves across his face, something I can't identify.

You're still lovely, he says.

I don't respond, then. I turn away from him and walk through the living room, through the kitchen, and out the front door.

Outside, it begins to rain. A soft gray drizzle that makes gentle plashes against the flagstones. I don't worry about locking the door, or about taking a set of keys. I know that when I return the door will be unlocked, and he will be here, waiting for me.

My ex once told me that I hold on to things too tightly. When we fought, he complained that I kept score, that I maintained a catalog of past slights from which it was impossible to return. It's true that I do hold a grudge, and my memory is excellent.

I think it's because I gave up painting that I keep holding on to it. Because I never allowed myself to truly fail, I keep imagining the artist I could have become. The dramatic severing of my practice, after what happened between me and the old painter, and that I never went back, that I never saw a way to go back—I think it was a way to keep that alternate self alive.

Because I no longer believed in myself, I didn't try. But that kept possible a world in which I did. The world where I did get what I wanted.

I wonder where my ex lives now. When he moved, he didn't leave a forwarding address. His mail continued to pile up in the box in our apartment building, and though I offered to drop it off somewhere for him, he never responded. I imagine it's piling up still.

I've taken the old painter's raincoat on my walk. He never wears it, so maybe it isn't his; maybe it was left by a guest. Or an old lover. It hangs on a hook with the other coats in the entrance to the house, yellow and rubberized. The sleeves are too long for my arms, and I roll them up. The falling rain forms a fine mist over my vision as I walk through the tall grasses down to the dock.

Not long after my ex and I began dating, we went to see a show on the Lower East Side. It was a solo show of paintings by a young queer artist who had recently emerged onto the contemporary scene, and I remember the gallery was especially busy that day. It was winter; everyone was wearing a dark, heavy coat, and our footsteps tracked in pinkish salt from the sidewalks. Because of our wet coats, we stood apart from each other, alone or in pairs, each of us encircled by a small, impermeable boundary, waiting for our turn to step forward and look at the work.

The paintings were large figural pieces on what seemed to be unprimed canvases. Bodies arced and swooped, the colors bright, sometimes even neon; paint dripped and rolled across the works' surfaces. The figures—they were women, some of them embracing, some of them so entwined they looked to be tangled together—were exaggerated, their shapes fleshy and elastic. Some of the figures reminded me of Senga Nengudi's pantyhose sculptures—stretched, visceral, as if they might snap into a different configuration once freed from the canvas. The images were built up in washes of paint, both thickly and thinly laid; some areas were masked off, tight and precise, while in others the paint was allowed to flow freely. I could sense the joy with which the paintings were made, and how fully the artist was in control of her material.

I remember saying this, not all of it, but much of it, in a long, semi-coherent burst to my ex, who at the time was neither my ex nor

my boyfriend; I was excited by the paintings, by the use of the medium, which seemed so playful and unexpected, wet instead of dry,
sensual instead of reserved. At one painting I stood for a long time,
tracking with my eyes the shape of each mark, trying to make sense of
what each layer consisted of and when it had been applied. When I
was done looking and thought I understood the process that the artist
had undergone, I found that my ex had left the gallery and was waiting for me outside.

After, when we sat down to eat at a Thai restaurant not far from
the gallery, he remarked on my response. He had appreciated the
show, too, but he hadn't been so enamored; was there something special in my knowledge of painting, or did I just love it that much?

I used to paint a little, I said.

I wanted to tell him that I had almost gotten my MFA, that I had
been really serious about it, once; I could feel the words in my mouth,
but to tell him would mean telling him why I stopped. I'd feared his
judgment of me, a fear that turned out to be a prescient one, and I had
wanted badly at that time to be cherished and loved. When I was
young, I said instead. I really got into it for a few years.

It was no secret to him that I was an arts writer, and seeing shows
would become a large part of what we did together. But that was the
first moment I hid a part of myself from him, and in time that part of
me grew closed over, even to myself, like a fist.

I had loved that person, the person I became with Colin, the person I became with my ex. I loved her critic's poise, her cool reserve,
the elegant way she smoked cigarettes and opened bottles with the flat
end of a Bic. I had loved becoming her, listening to her music, wearing her clothes, as I altered myself, changing my story, which I saw as
an act of agency then, and which I think now was an act of survival.

At the dock, I unlatch the gate from the inside and step through, my shoes squeaking on the wet wood. Slowly I walk down to the water. The rain is falling into the ocean; it looks like it just disappears. Both boats, the speedboat and the rowboat, the skiff, are moored at the dock. They bob gently in the ebb and swell of the waves. The ropes tethering them are green and ancient, and when I touch one I expect wet streaks of algae to come off on my skin. But it's not slippery; it's rough, and leaves a dank, mildewy smell on my hand.

Each of the boats looks in working order, not that I can really tell. They're clean, no rust on them, hardly any grime. The rowboat has a name, hand-painted on the inside of its sky-blue hull: *PUCK*. Block letters, no serifs. It has two seats. Rainwater has pooled inside and slides around on the bottom of the boat, a transparent, embryonic shape, droplets breaking apart and coming back together again.

The first day I arrived in Maine, I dressed as though I were still in the city or on tour, as though I were in a place where people might see and form judgments of me. I'd packed for my trip knowing I would be seen, bringing my plissé trousers and filmy dresses, garments I usually loved to wear and that brought me great confidence. Since then, though, since agreeing to stay at the old painter's house, I've dressed lazily, even sloppily, wearing the same oversize sweater and athletic leggings every day. My book-tour clothes hang in the guest room closet, unworn. If he's noticed my decline in presentation, the old painter hasn't mentioned it. He doesn't own a full-length mirror, not one that I have access to, and the only sight I've had of myself in three days has been in the small vanity mirror above the guest bathroom sink, its surface desilvered and gone black in places with age. All of this, this laxity around my dress, the impossibility of seeing myself all in one piece, has reduced my sense of physical self to an amorphous blob. I am certain that I exist where I can see myself; I am

not certain that I exist anywhere else. Here on the dock, the rain in my
hair, misting my skin, I feel see-through, without outline, no more
consequential than the raindrop that, falling from such great height,
encounters and rejoins the sea.

The speedboat, which is painted a handsome burgundy and
cream, bright even on this dreary day, is big enough to hold two pas-
sengers, maybe three. I look for its name and find it, painted in script
on the side—also hand-done, in two colors, one for the text and another for a highlight. *Julie*. A flourish on the *J* that extends and turns
into an underline. I'm disappointed by this, by the old painter's pre-
dictable misogyny. I don't know that I expected better from him—
maybe *better* isn't the word, maybe I mean *more*, imaginatively—but
I make a note to ask him who Julie is, or was. To him.

Like the rowboat, *Julie* is clean and well kept. I wonder when he
goes to maintain the boats, or if there's someone he's hired to do it for
him. Maybe he takes care of them when he goes swimming, before he
dives into the water. Maybe he looks at them, looks at *Julie*, waiting
for the fog, the heavy gray sky, to lift.

On a whim, I go to the edge of the dock. I could step into the
speedboat now, and I do, lowering myself gingerly into the pilot's
seat. There's a steering wheel and dials, buttons; none of it means
anything to me. I wouldn't know how to start the motor if asked. Still,
there is something exhilarating about just sitting here, tethered as the
boat is, feeling the ceaseless motion of the sea.

I notice a ladder going off the side of the boat, too, metal with
white plastic rungs. The old painter must take the boat out on nice
days, slip off the edge for a swim.

Some weeks after we went to the Christina Quarles show, I realized I had left my scarf at the Thai restaurant. I called and they said
they didn't have it; I called the gallery, and they didn't have it, either.

I was disconsolate, disproportionately so. My ex said that I shouldn't worry about it, that I could buy another scarf, a nicer one. But I didn't want another one; I wanted the one that had been mine. The same day we went to the Quarles show, we ran into a former colleague of mine on the street. He hadn't been my direct supervisor, but I had had to work with him frequently, and I'd found him to be a brusque, insensitive man who gave me a hard time about my writing. When he saw me on the street, he smiled widely, and greeted me as though I were an old friend. It was because I had come up in the world, I thought, and was therefore elevated in his opinion; I responded to him coolly, and after, my ex said that I could have been nicer to him, that he had seemed happy to see me. I explained about our previous work relationship, that I didn't feel the need to treat him kindly, and my ex repeated that I still could have been kind to him, it would have cost me nothing.

Yes, I hold on to things too tightly. But I have let things go; I have let so many things go. Losing farther, losing faster. I know how to let things go, how to release my grip and say goodbye. It's that I don't know when.

Some weeks after I'd lost my scarf, something scary happened to me and my ex, an event that brought us together. Throughout our entire relationship it was the memory of that harrowing event, and the fact that we had experienced it together, that connected us and made us feel as though we shared an unbreakable bond. Then that relationship ended. I hadn't thought it would.

I clamber out of the boat—it's harder than I think, and I have to brace myself, one hand on its edge, then a foot, before propelling myself up and out—and *Julie* stirs, troubled by my spastic movements. But the ropes remain fast, and soon the frantic knocking turns into a gentle bob, and then it's as if I were never there.

When I return from my walk, it's later than usual, dusk already beginning to color the sky. The old painter is sitting at the kitchen table.

I didn't want to eat without you, he says.

There are two plates on the table, which is set with forks and knives, like an illustration in a children's book. He looks weary.

You should have gone to bed, I say.

I wanted to wait for you, he repeats.

After dinner, in my room—it's not my room but it's my room—I strip out of my walking clothes and put on the dress that I wore to the department dinner in Iowa, the evening after I met Zoë. There's a zipper that begins low in the small of my back, and when I slowly pull it up, I feel the nakedness of my body underneath, briefly awake to the gap between silk and skin. Reaching to adjust the straps of the dress, I catch a whiff of my own scent. The open hollow of my armpit where sweat has pooled.

I look at myself in the darkened window, the reeds waving through my reflection. Run my fingers through my hair, tuck a lock behind my ear. Wonder if the woman I was will return to me. But the harder I try to become her, the harder the image resists.

I imagine someone on the opposite shore, looking this way, seeing my lit-up window. If they saw me standing here, what would they think?

Then I draw the curtains shut and change into my shapeless clothes again.

Who's Julie, I ask the old painter the next morning.

He's sealing an envelope, carefully pressing the flap shut. He tests the adhesive with his thumbnail before responding.

You found the boats, he says.

Was she a girlfriend? I ask. Or your mother?

Not my mother, no, he says, wincing. My first girlfriend.

Ah, I say. Did you meet in high school? I ask. Did she break your heart and ruin you for all following girlfriends?

What? No, he says. He sets the envelope down, next to his mug of coffee. We met in college. We dated for three years and were hoping to get married but she died very suddenly during her senior year of a massive brain bleed.

God, I say. I'm sorry.

I cannot stop being cruel to him and it shames me.

It was a long time ago, he says.

What was she like?

She was very gentle, he answers. Blond, very light blond hair, like wheat in the sun. She was studying medicine. But, he says, as though he already knows I'm trying to picture her and failing, anything I tell you about her won't describe her properly.

He gets up to pour more coffee and when he comes back I say, You never married. That was the mythology around you in school, that you were a perpetual bachelor.

Yes, he says. Though it wasn't entirely true. I was married once. It only lasted a year.

When was that?

In my early thirties. The marriage was so short I hardly told anyone about it.

What happened?

He takes a sip, frowning slightly. Nothing happened. It wasn't the right decision for either of us, and we realized that after a few months.

Why wasn't it the right decision?

I shouldn't have been married, he answers. I wasn't good at taking care of the relationship. My work was always more important.

Were you kind to her?

No, he says. Not always.

I'm trying to imagine the women of the old painter's life, but all I can conjure is a line of women in old-fashioned white dresses, like figures in a Pre-Raphaelite painting. And then me.

Were there others? I ask, and I know that he knows what I'm asking.

Are you jealous, now? he says, but there's no heat in it.

No, I say, I just want to know.

Yes, he says. Though fewer than you'd think.

While I was your student?

None then, he says. Just—

Just me, I say.

He sighs. Retreats to the living room. He's started a new canvas; the underpainting is washes of burnt umber. The blunt, rocky shapes of an island are blocked out along the horizon.

Yes, he says.

I could ask him then, why he did it, why he chose me, but I find I don't want to. I stand and leave him with his easel; I've left the book I started reading in my room, and I want to finish it.

———

That night I decide to make dinner. I've noticed that the old painter's energy becomes depleted in the evenings, though he tries to hide it.

Since my arrival he has given me free rein in the kitchen; the fridge is stocked with groceries he orders from the mainland and from the small store on the island. Someone—a young man, a seasonal summer worker of the sort who seem to be everywhere on these islands—leaves them on the front step of the house.

The old painter's kitchen is more beautiful, more expansive than any kitchen in any house in which I've lived. The countertops have the luster of oiled wood; the knives have sharpened Japanese blades. Turning one on end, balancing its point on the cutting board, I see that at the base of the knife's handle is a carved character, like a Chinese seal; it leaves its mirrored shape on my fingertip when I press against it. When I stand at the sink, rinsing my hands, feeling the heavy pressure of the water from the tap, I understand that this is what his privilege affords him, and me by extension, as his guest.

I'm making chicken from a recipe I found on the internet. It calls for garlic, shallots, and grapes. I'm prepping everything, standing at the counter, while the old painter sits in his chair.

I hear him lean forward as I split a head of garlic, popping cloves onto the cutting board.

Do I anger you, Christine? he says.

I don't stop what I'm doing. One by one, I smash the garlic cloves with the flat of my knife.

No, I say. Not anymore.

I slice the end of each clove and begin to peel off the papery skins.

Why did you kill me in your book? the old painter asks.

I keep working, not answering him. Some of the skins cleave away easily; others are stickier, I have to lift them with my fingernail from where they cling to the cloves. I can feel the slight tackiness of the garlic on my fingertips. Then I am done and a pile of garlic skins, delicate as flower petals, has accumulated on the cutting board.

Because I wanted to punish you, I say.

Hmm, he says. And what do you want from me now?

I want to understand you, I answer.

And what will help you with that?

I rinse my hands under the faucet and take out the chicken, which is halved and wrapped in butcher paper. Peel back the paper to reveal the soft, translucent flesh with its layer of fatty yellow skin. I remove the cleaver from where it's stored in a drawer and with my palm pressed against the dull edge I use my weight to break down the chicken into pieces. Each joint snaps with a sickening crunch. I know we're both listening.

Why did you do it? I say.

There's no heat in my voice, but my hands are shaking.

Do what?

I needed a mentor, I say. Not—whatever it was.

A lover, he says.

You weren't my lover, I say. You know that.

The day he had asked me to come to the mountains with him, I returned home to a freezing apartment. I thought perhaps my room-mate had turned the heat down before leaving for break, assuming I'd be out of town too. But when I turned the thermostat as high as it went the radiators remained silent, and when I ran the shower the water came out as cold as ice.

Unbeknownst to my roommate and me, our heating bill had been attached to that of the unit below us; when our downstairs neighbor moved out, closing her various accounts, the gas company responded by turning off the building's heat. My roommate, who handled our utilities and who in fact was the sole person on our lease, was already back home by then; when I called her, she said she'd try to sort it out but it was hard, she was with family, and anyway it was possible that the gas company wouldn't be able to come right away to fix it. Would I be able to find a place to stay, she asked; I said I would.

I hadn't thought of my life as shabby or precarious at the time, though it had been both of those things. I didn't know my roommate well; like me, she was rarely home, and as a result of our negligence the apartment was barely furnished. Scuff marks from previous tenants remained on the walls, and all the windows faced north, so only a weak, winterish sunlight appeared for a few hours each morning. We had a couch, a coffee table, a television I never learned how to use, and a flimsy two-person table at which we ate dinner, never at the same time.

In my room, off the phone with my roommate, I exhaled and my breath fogged white. I flexed my fingers and they were stiff, almost painful. I considered my options: to stay in the apartment, to call a friend—I didn't have any friends in that town—or to go to the mountains with the old painter. I thought, fleetingly, of sleeping in the studio, on the futon I kept rolled up in my painting nook. But I couldn't bear the thought of being discovered, like a squatter, living illicitly on university grounds, and what was it that I was so afraid of, anyhow? I could go on this trip with him. It was being offered so freely.

When I remember this moment now, I can only see, with clarity, how young I was then. And there was nothing wrong with being that young: My only recourse was to try to enjoy it, the same way as anyone. What the old painter offered me was an adult experience, a way to skip over all the dinginess, a glimpse of living like the people who were already successful and well loved. He had already shown me as much in the dinners and parties he hosted, events at which I chattered with the other graduate students and dressed as they dressed. He didn't know what my apartment looked like when I came home, dumping my clothes onto the floor into a heap; he didn't know how delinquently I lived.

My hands were cold enough that I had trouble using my phone; the screen wouldn't respond, and I placed four fingers in the cave of my mouth, exhaling to warm them until the touchscreen worked. Then I called and told him yes, I would come and meet him in P——.

I had known, even then, that what would happen could happen. I had been afraid of, and I had also been excited by, that stark glimmer of risk and possibility, the kind of excitement that has no positive or negative valence, only intensity. I had packed knowing this, not daring to imagine it. What had I brought: Black tights, running my palm along the inside of each pair to check for ladders. Lace-trimmed underwear, nylon-blend panties in shades of pink and red that I didn't realize would be visible through my stockings. A black dress that was both too short and too tight. A black wool peacoat that was both trendy and out of style at the same time. Heeled black boots that laced up, boots that weren't meant for the cold and let the wind in. I wouldn't be able to wear them in the snow. Yet they were the only shoes I thought to bring.

I spent just one night in my apartment. The landlord, taking pity on our situation, came to drop off a pair of electric radiators, from which ebbed a pallid, yellow-gray heat. I wound myself in blankets until only my face peeped out, plugged in one radiator next to me, and slept fitfully, my vision spotted with stars.

In the morning, I walked to the train station, where I took the train to P——. I couldn't hold a single thought in my head the entire train ride; I desperately wanted to sleep, but I was afraid of missing my stop, and when I did nod off I was woken an hour later by the conductor, who gently shook my shoulder and pointed to the station sign outside. I became anxious then, it moved through my body in cold pulses, and my heart hammered in my throat. I was certain the old painter would not be waiting for me, that it would turn out I had imagined the whole thing.

Yet he was there, waiting in a dark coat, and when he saw me he raised one hand. I went to him, breathless, face shocked from the cold. Come, he said, and took my bag from me, and we walked away together.

It occurs to me now that we must have looked startling, salacious, my naked youth and his reserved gray—at that age I had no idea how anything looked to outsiders, only how it felt. Try as I might, I can't remember being watched, can't remember any whispers, though at the time those would have excited me too. It's possible that even our imbalance looked utterly ordinary to other people, and no one cared. There our weekend began.

I wash my hands, turn on the stove, place the cast-iron on the burner and wait for it to heat.

After we got back, I say. That spring, that first critique of mine— why didn't you stand up for me?

Stand up for you? he says. Christine, you know why. Those paintings were awful.

I know they were, I say. But—

I wasn't going to lie to you, he says, and I wasn't going to embarrass myself in front of my colleagues.

So you embarrassed me instead.

That's not true.

After that weekend you never called. You practically disappeared.

You're sounding like a scorned lover, Christine.

Stop saying my name like that, I snap at him. You don't get to have it both ways—you can't call me your lover and then act surprised when I have expectations of you. Had, I say.

Did you think I had a responsibility to you after we slept together? Kind of, I say. Yes. You did.

I pass my hand under the faucet, flick a few drops of water into the pan to see if it's ready.

Tell me, he says, and I turn, quickly, to see if he's teasing me, but his face is serious.

No, I say. You tell me. Tell me why you did it. Tell me why you fucked me.

He winces.

I uncork the olive oil, drizzle a generous amount into the pan. It spatters where the water hasn't yet evaporated.

You chose me, I say. You taught me, and you fed me. And then you asked me to go to a place with you, and I said yes.

I drop the garlic cloves into the pan, swirling them with a wooden spatula.

I thought you were talented, he says. And I thought you were beautiful. Of course I did. Oh, Christine. You must have known that.

I knew, I say.

A sweeping, sickening regret crashes over me then, and I have to keep the tears out of my voice. But I still thought I was worth more to you than that.

He's quiet. I place the pieces of meat in the pan, one at a time. The fat spits, hisses against the cast-iron.

What hurt the most, I say, wasn't that you left, or that you didn't take me seriously as a lover. It was that, after everything that happened, I couldn't believe in myself as an artist anymore, not without thinking about what else you had wanted from me. And what you took. Every critique, every word of praise, all of it died in the shadow of what happened between us. I couldn't paint after that weekend, Richard. I lost it completely, and I've never been able to get it back.

I place the shallots in the hot pan, then the grapes. Some of them burst immediately, filling the room with a winey sweetness.

He stands, Richard. Comes to me in the kitchen. He places one hand on my back—I don't flinch, somehow I've expected it—and bows his head.

I shouldn't have, he says.

It's a poor apology.

No, I say. You shouldn't.

MAINE

The sun is in my eyes. When I shade my vision with one hand, the sea appears perfectly round, extending in every direction. Only the humped shapes of the other islands, far on the horizon, suggest there is other life here.

Richard, in his windbreaker, is piloting the boat. He's really thin now, new air between his neck and shoulders, deeper creases in his cheeks. The smell of motor oil, as he revs the engine, pierces the air. Beneath it is the dark-green marine smell of the ocean, kelpy, mineral. It's a beautiful day. I've been in Maine for nearly three weeks. Last night, he couldn't stop vomiting. He wouldn't let me in to help, even though I could hear him through his bedroom door, retching. After, he went to the kitchen and I gave him a glass of water. I hope this death doesn't rob me of all my dignity, he said, in a casual way, and I didn't know what to say so I took the glass from him and refilled it.

He is happy here, I can see. Happy on the water. Though I know he is in pain he moves fluidly, easily around the cockpit, his sturdy, knobby hands familiar with the boat's controls. Maybe that's why I ask him what I've been wondering, another thing I've wanted to ask him.

Richard, I say. How do you want to die?

Spray of salt in the air. He surfs us over the waves for a while, so long that I think he hasn't heard me. Then he cuts the engine and answers.

Much like this, I think.

Like this?

On a nice day. At sea. Peacefully.

I could push you over the edge now, I offer.

No thanks, he says. That wouldn't be very peaceful.

I've always been afraid of drowning, I say.

Me too, he answers.

We float along in silence. The sound of the ocean is endless, waves upon waves. Water laps at the edge of the boat; I think I can reach it with my hand, but I can't. Looking around, at the expanse of sea, I feel that my eyes have become saturated with beauty. The quiet of this place seems to have stilled me, made me receptive. To everything.

Christine, he says now, and I look over to him.

Do you still want to kill me?

=

Afternoon. I'm cooking for us again. Though I don't know if he'll eat. There's sauce simmering on the stove, half an onion surrounded

by canned tomatoes, a lump of butter melted in. I stir the sauce occasionally, sliding the onion around so that it doesn't stick to the pan. It
turns out that I like having something to do with my hands, something removed from language. But I knew this. My notebooks and
laptop have remained shut ever since I arrived. Richard is by the windows, backlit, working on a new painting.

His hand has grown looser and looser, the colors still close to life,
with a few startling accents—that caustic edge that I recall from his
main body of work. The paint is totally liquid; it flows across the canvas in layered washes. If I didn't know they were seascapes I'd think
they were something else.

Your retrospective, I say. In the city.

It had gone up in late spring. A month after my book came out. I
had seen the reviews in the paper, the color postcards, in fact it'd been
impossible to avoid them. At the time I'd thought, vengefully, that it
had been timed to disturb me, right when I was trying to bury his
ghost. I'd thought, too, that the show seemed oddly placed, when as
far as I knew he was still alive and well and making work.

Richard lifts his head at my voice. He's starting to look scruffy;
his buzz cut requires maintenance. Tufts of hair are growing straight
out of his head, making him look owlish and disheveled.

Yes?

I saw that it was happening, I say. It seemed like a big deal. I didn't
see it, I add, before he asks.

I wouldn't think you would.

You had already moved out here by then. For years.

That's right.

Was it— I can't figure out how to phrase it. Was it because you
knew you were sick?

How observant. Yes. I did call my gallerist, once I found out. She

was shocked, distraught, wanted to call all the papers and tell them
my tragic tale. I didn't let her, of course.

But you did allow for publicity.

In the interviews I'd read, his quotes had been evasive. Summary.
At times hagiographic and past tense. He'd spoken like a man writing
his own eulogy.

Of course, he says again. But I didn't want anyone's pity.

What did you want from all of it?

The show? Or my life?

The show. Both, I say.

The sauce bubbles, spattering tomato onto the back of my hand. I
taste it, turn down the heat, stir it again.

From the show—I wanted to sell a ton of work. Don't look at me
like that, Christine. You must have realized that I'm a bourgeois capi-
talist like the rest. And I'm dying, I wanted to be rid of it. The other
thing I wanted was for museums to acquire the work. As many as
possible.

Spreading your seed, I say.

Don't be vulgar. Anyway, it worked, though there weren't as
many acquisitions as I'd hoped.

I think about telling him that I saw a postcard with his painting
on it in Chicago. How something of his had found me, even then.
But I don't, though I know it would please him. Instead, I imagine
his gallerist—I picture a flaxen-haired woman who looks exactly as
I've imagined Julie, his first girlfriend—cannily calling up museums,
alluding to how his work will appreciate in value. Soon, I imagine her
saying. Soon. But that must be a balm for him. Knowing that his work
lives on in a collection, that years from now, or decades, it might be
mounted in a show. With his name printed next to it, and his dates of
birth and death.

Is that also what you wanted of your life?

He turns his gimlet eye on me.

Don't we all want to make something that outlives us?

We?

My paintings. Your book. We're not so different.

I didn't write my novel to become immortal, I say.

No. Merely to set the record straight.

That wasn't why I wrote it either, I say.

But he settles back into his chair, picking up his brush, and I know he thinks he's won.

I fill a pot with water. So heavy, the pressure from this tap; it doesn't take long. Then I put it on the stove and turn on the heat.

I didn't write the book to settle a score. No. But I wrote it, and when it was done, I asked for it to enter the world.

The moment where it changed—where the writing went from a process of trying to understand what had happened to me to a process of creating something new—occurred not during the first draft, or even the second, but the third. It was when I started to think of it as a book in earnest, to sculpt it, pulling a form out from my life's shapeless contours. It was when I started to make it into something striking, fearsome and beautiful. Then the book had lifted off the ground and become suspended in midair, and all the ascending glass steps had followed.

I had wanted to write a good book. I had wanted to make it sharp, readable, and deadly. I had wanted to make it scream. I'd been so angry—so angry at Richard, so angry at myself—when I began the project. But by the end, when the book was done and I found it clean and whole, without seam or flaw, I felt nothing but light. It had fully separated from me then, a parasite freed from its host. I'd thought only that I had made something good, and I was proud of my effort.

I lift the lid of the pot. Tiny bubbles are starting to form; the heat makes the water swirl, like a mirage in the desert. Richard's words resonate in my head.

If we are to die. If we all are to die. Is that why, then, we make all this?

Once, after a bad crit, Frances and I sat together on the floor of her studio. When you really think about it, she said, there's no point to any of this. She was holding a brush in her hand, splaying the bristles against her palm. We're just making shapes on walls in rooms.

That's not true, I said, though at the time I didn't disagree with her. Art matters, I said. The words felt false in my mouth. It matters that we make things.

I know it's supposed to matter, Frances said. She bent the brush against her hand, almost violently.

Frances, stop, I said, you'll ruin it.

She lifted the brush and the bristles sprang back. She stroked them into shape, reverently. I don't think art has to have a point, she said. The thing is that we keep doing it. That we have to.

After I'd finished my study of Frances, the first and only time she sat for me, she slipped off the stool right away to look at the painting.

Weird, she said, wrinkling her nose.

What?

It's so me, she said.

Yeah, well. It is you.

I could tell she was pleased.

I love it, she said. You saw me.

For the rest of the afternoon we were in the studio together, I saw her eyes keep lifting to the painting. That, more than anything, let me know that I had made something good.

I included the portrait of Frances in our thesis show, and when it came down I wrapped it and gave it to her. I don't know if she still has it. For a while, during the years that we weren't speaking, I would study the backgrounds of the photos she posted, wondering if it might appear on a wall or in a room. At first I had felt sad at the thought of her getting rid of the painting. Then I realized that the important part was already over, which was the act of its making.

For years I had tried to rationalize to myself that there was something useful about art, that it solved social problems, that it contributed to the good of the world. If I could twist and re-form my own desires to fit through these argumentative hoops, it made what I was pursuing feel less selfish and lightweight. But I think Frances was right: There doesn't need to be a point. It's not rational, this desire to make things. But it is real.

My mother, years ago, asked me why I wanted to be an artist.

Because it made me happy, I told her, and I loved it.

Was that enough?

It was. It is.

The water is boiling, the lid rattles, steam hissing out. I toss in a heavy dose of salt, add the long sheaf of pasta, egg-yellow and translucent. In the living room, Richard sets down his brush and stretches. The canvas is completely saturated with color. Runny blues and greens, a whisper of lilac. Thick blocks of titanium white streak across the top of the painting—

Clouds, he says, when he sees me looking.

It's beautiful, I say.

My dealer doesn't know about these, he says. They're my secret paintings.

I'm right here, I want to say, but I don't say anything.

He leaves to change out of his painting clothes and when he comes back I have something else to ask him.

In all those years, I say. Were you ever written up?

No, he says, no one did anything.

But there were reports? Or rumors?

No, I don't think so.

So no one cared that it happened?

I didn't say that.

So you were never disciplined.

No, he says, I wasn't. Why? Are you trying to punish me now?

No, I say.

The pasta's done; I take it out with a pair of tongs, swirl it through the sauce. The tomatoes, simmering, have cooked down, silky and savory from the melted butter. I put a portion on my plate, then reach for his.

Are you going to eat? I ask him.

No, he says.

I add his portion to mine instead; I have an appetite.

=

That evening, Richard keeps fussing with his hair. When he catches sight of himself, reflected in the tall windows, he frowns. He's always been vain. There's no barber on the island, he tells me.

How often do you cut it?

Every two weeks, he answers. I suppose I'll leave it.

I'll do it for you, I say.

Neither of us expects that I will say this.

Well, he says. Sure. There's clippers here.

To get to the bathroom, I have to walk through his room with him, which I thought I wouldn't want to do. But it is cleaner and more neutral than I expect. His sheets are white and the bed is made, the corners neat, sheets pulled taut. Boarding school, he says, when he sees me looking. Aside from the nightstand, which is covered with amber prescription bottles of varying size, his room is ordinary. Empty, almost, like a monk's cell.

In his bathroom we both pretend we don't see the medical paraphernalia scattered about, most of which he has been given by his palliative care team, whose calls he has been ignoring for the past week. He's not using much of it, except for the pain pills. In the cabinet under the sink there's a black plastic box with a trimmer and various blade attachments. When I open it, a faint scent of pomade and hair grease. Gray hairs cling to the edges of the blade guards. One, the second shortest, seems to be the one he's used most often. I remember that he liked, likes to wear his hair that way. Neat and close.

Well, he says. He sits on the lid of the toilet, leaning forward slightly, and he looks so old and pathetic that I suddenly feel winded. He's given me too much power.

No, I say. Not there. I can't reach behind you.

Where, then, he says.

There's a shower chair he's too proud to use, a pile of pamphlets stacked on top. *Holistic Practices in Palliative Care. Managing Your Pain.* I clear it and place it in the middle of the bathroom. Here, I say. I try not to notice how he grips the handles on either side of the plastic seat.

He closes his eyes when I turn the clippers on, before I even bring them to his skin. The noise is loud, vibrating off the tile. I move slowly, my fingertips gently touching him, one hand cupping the side of his head. Up the nape of his neck, then around his head, moving upward in shallow strokes. I've given haircuts like this before, to the men in my life. I know how to do it, to not be frightened by the sound or the blade. When I go around his ear, I use two fingers to press it down, the cartilaginous shell of it, pink with blood, and I see the freckles there, from decades of sun exposure. He must have come here every summer, once he bought this house.

Ah, he says, his voice thick.

Am I hurting you?

No, he says. It just feels strange.

To be touched.

Yes.

I do the other side of his head, then switch the guard to a longer one to do the top. My fingertips graze over his scalp, and I can smell him, that oily, human, top-of-the-head smell, and I realize I know it, I've been smelling him the entire time I've been in his house. It's strange I didn't recognize it. But there had always been so much between us, so much noise and material between me and him, before. I take off the guard to use the bare blade to clean up his hairline. It does scare me, a little, to see the strip of untanned skin exposed, and how close I've cut.

He is wearing a black T-shirt, and when I am done he looks as though he has been dusted with snow, or ash. He looks clean, too, trim again, younger and older at the same time. Less like a madman.

He turns to check his reflection in the mirror over the sink.

It's good, he says.

You're welcome. I bend down to unplug the clippers and he catches the inside of my elbow with his hand.

Christine, he says.

He moves his hand up my arm, then tilts his palm, grazing my chest. I can feel the heat of his hand through my shirt, and I don't move. Shame and disgust flood through my body, white-hot, burning my cheeks.

Richard, I say. No.

I pull the cord out of the wall.

Worth a try, he says, letting his hand drop.

You're disgusting, I say.

I feel him watching as I pack the clipper and guards back into the hard plastic case. His gray eyes follow my every move. I thrust the case back under the sink, then rise and wash my hands.

You're free to leave if you want to, he says. But his voice falters, is weak instead of strong. It's not a challenge, it's a question, and we both know I won't. There's still something I need from him, something I want to take from him, something that keeps me here.

In our reflections in the mirror I can see how time has moved through each of us. At some point in the last decade I started thinking of myself as a woman, not a girl. It's this woman I see in the mirror, tall and lean, standing over him.

Good night, Richard, I say. I leave him sitting in the middle of the bathroom, his hands in his lap, palms facing toward the ceiling.

If I really wanted to hurt him, I could. I could destroy all his remaining work, like my character does in the novel; I know where the knives are kept. I could flush his pain pills down the toilet. I could set his house on fire. I could, when he's sleeping, steal into his room, and press a pillow over his face. But I haven't.

In the book, when I kill him, it happens off the page. Suspended as I was in the authorial seat, I still couldn't imagine how it would feel.

Later that night, I hear him on a call. I can't make out what he's saying, only bits and pieces of conversation. His tone is serious, and I wonder if he's speaking to his gallerist. Or maybe it's someone else—his doctor? I press my ear to the door of my room, listening.

  —*Good, so it's authorized—yes—I'll pick it up—*

I press my ear so hard against the door that I think the wood grain must be imprinting itself into my skin, but I can't make out anything else. When I step away from the wall, my ear is smashed and sore, and I massage it with the cool fingers of one hand, willing the blood back in.

         =

Morning, early, weak gray light filtering through the clouds. I'm in the living room, reading, when he comes to me, rubbing a towel roughly around his head. He's still been going for his daily swim, though I have no idea how he manages it. I've stopped watching him; I don't know if he still swims to the buoy and back.

  Let's go on a little trip today, he says.

  Where?

  He doesn't answer. He vigorously tips his head in one direction, tapping against his ear with the towel. Getting the water out, he says, as if that's the explanation I'm demanding.

  Where are we going, I say again.

  Get dressed, he says, we'll have to catch the ferry.

  We take his car onto the ferry and spend the boat ride on the observation deck. I sit on one of the gritty white benches while he stands. The tooth of the concrete pokes through the stretchy fabric of my leggings. When a gust swells over the water I turn up the collar of my sweater, but Richard points his face in the direction of the wind. He looks invigorated, agitated. When the ferry docks, he roars out of the

parking lot, speeding through Rockport to get to the highway. Once
on the road, he tells me where we're headed.

We're going to the pharmacist, he says.

I feel a sudden lightness, the way you feel when you get into an
elevator and it descends.

In Brunswick, we stop for lunch at a roadside stand that serves fried
hot dogs. He orders two for himself and one for me. The sausage is
red and fried to a crisp, and when I bite into it, my mouth fills with
grease. Richard is animated, talking as he eats, waving around his
hands. I'm reminded of how he behaved at the department receptions,
his grandiosity after two glasses of wine. He seems happy; I think
he is.

I used to come here with Julie, he says. He puts one hand on the
plastic picnic table. Nothing's changed.

A few miles later we have to pull over so he can throw up on the
side of the road.

Don't look at me.

I wasn't.

He wipes his mouth and yanks the door shut.

I can drive, I say, but he tells me he's fine, and he is dying, so I let
him.

In the car, he suddenly says:

How long have you been single, Christine?

Don't ask me that, I say. Then, because I want to know what he's
sensed about me, I say, How did you know?

Because you came.

That doesn't mean anything.

People in loving relationships don't travel thousands of miles to confront people they think have wronged them.

Fine, I say. That's not what I'm doing here, for the record.

No, it's not, he agrees, and he doesn't ask further.

His remark has tugged something loose in me, and I find myself telling him about what happened between me and my ex. He listens, his gray eyes trained on the road, and when I am done, he says:

So you lied to him about who you were.

That's not what I did.

You pretended to be someone else. Because you were ashamed of what happened?

Because I didn't know how to speak about it.

And so you hid part of yourself from him.

What, that you fucked me?

No, he says. That you're an artist.

I don't know what to say to that, so I don't say anything.

We drive in silence, and I look out the window, watching the land-scape scroll past. As we're nearing the pharmacy, he suddenly speaks again.

I want to leave the house to you, he says.

Don't, I say.

He pulls in to the parking spot. Turns off the engine.

There's no one else it would go to.

I don't want to live there.

It's not about what you do or don't want. Come on, he says.

He's standing outside the car now, waiting for me, and like so many other times in my life, I rise and follow him.

After we pick up the prescription, Richard is tired. When I offer to drive, he doesn't protest, and we switch. I barely have to adjust the position of the driver's seat. Meanwhile, he leans the passenger seat as far back as it will go and closes his eyes.

Just for a minute, he says.

Okay, I say.

He is holding the white paper bag from the pharmacy cradled in his lap. The top has been folded over twice and stapled shut. Inside are three powders that, when mixed with water and ingested, will stop his heart after putting him to sleep. When I merge onto the highway, picking up speed, I can hear the hollow rattling of the bag, moving against his hands.

The drive is straightforward and scenic and at many points we go over water, on narrow two-lane bridges. As Richard sleeps, the vibration of the car emphasizes the slackness of his skin. His mouth is slightly open, and I think he's dreaming of something because expressions keep flickering across his face.

It's too painful to look at him like this, so I keep my eyes on the road, glancing over at him occasionally to see if he's asleep or awake. It's a long drive home, and I want to turn on the radio, but I don't want to wake him, and so I spend it in silence, with only my own thoughts for company.

He's still asleep when I drive us onto the ferry. I would leave him in the car if it weren't for the smell of gasoline and motor oil that fills the lower deck. I turn off the engine, unbuckle my seatbelt, and when I turn to wake him I'm struck by how close we are, suspended in the quiet container of the car. What is it that I feel—tenderness, confusion, and revulsion, all at once, close enough to touch the gray stubble on his cheeks, to smell his sour breath, to see where tears have formed in the inner corners of his eyes while he's slept. Then I do touch him, one hand on his face. I'm certain he will wake, but he doesn't stir, and I trace the line of his jaw with my hand. He's lost so much weight, but it's not just that. He's different from the man I knew, and I'm not certain if the shift occurred while I was here, or if it was before I came. I want to think that it's something to do with me. That I've changed him. Then I touch his shoulder, shake him until he blinks, gasps, his eyes impossibly far away until they focus on me, and I don't want to lose that gaze, I don't want to see his death.

Richard, I say, we're on the ferry, we're here.

The house is cool and dark when we return. The end of summer comes sooner this far north. Richard says something as he disappears into the kitchen, but I don't hear him, lost in thought as I am. I want to run away, away from him and what he's asked of me. It would be cruel of me to go, but I can't find a way to reconcile our opposing desires, and I have spent so much time here already being cruel.

He doesn't want to die alone, and I don't want to kill him.

I go to the living room, where his easel is. With my socks on I feel as though I'm gliding across the hardwood, weightless. He's left his brushes out, and his palette is still wet. I pick up a long-handled filbert. Imagine what it would be like to make a mark. Then to blot out the whole thing.

When he returns, he's no longer holding the bag from the pharmacy. He looks at me.

Painting again? he asks.

I set the brush back in its stand. No, I say. Thinking.

A small light appears in the window far behind the two of us, moving across the sky. It skims along the horizon, its path wavering, and vanishes.

He's left the medication in the kitchen. On the counter, as if it were a piece of mail.

=

That night, while he is sleeping, I take the paper bag from the pharmacy and tear it open, breaking the seals on each of the three bags of white powder. The texture of the first is soft and inert, like powdery snow, and I catch a few grains of it on my fingertip, the tiny granules squeaking slightly as they press against forefinger and thumb. I'm tempted to taste it, and the thought makes me hold both hands low and away from my body, where they can't reach my face. Then I tip each bag into the toilet and flush it, and once the bowl has refilled with water, I flush it again.

After, I wash my hands, scrubbing hard, looking at my reflection in the spotted mirror. I want to know what she's thinking. But the only woman before me is me.

=

He notices the medication is gone the next morning.

Christine, he says. He's standing in the entrance to the kitchen; I'm reading by the windows. I can see how slight he is, how he braces himself with one elbow against the doorframe.

Yes.

Where is it?

Where's what, I say. I close my book. Languidly.

Please don't joke around, he says. They won't give me another prescription, not even if I beg for it. What did you do with it, Christine?

I threw it out, I say.

Why on earth would you do that, he says. His voice now a thunderous growl.

Because I'm not going to help you, I say. Because that's what you want. And that's what you've always wanted. To use me. Because you know I'll come when you call, and I always have. But—

He's descending the steps to the living room, but I stay seated.

I'm not going to let you pull me into this, I say.

I thought this was what you wanted, he says. He stands over me. That you wanted your revenge. Don't you?

And I can see, now, that he's scared. That I've really taken something away from him. I'm filled—and I hate that I feel this way, but I feel it—with a sick, ugly pleasure. That I've ruined this.

Are you proud of yourself? he asks.

I keep my chin high, my posture straight. Defying him the only way I know how.

Christine, he says, his voice suddenly anguished. You don't know what it's like to die.

Yes, I want to say. Yes, I do, because I died when you turned your back on me. But I know, even as I want it to be true, that I would be lying. Because I know nothing of death. It's why I could only kill him in my book, why I can't do it in real life.

I'm crying, I realize. Hot, silent tears, sliding down my cheeks. But I don't say anything. I can't. I've taken away his good death.

=

Against both our expectations, I stay in the house. For two days, we don't speak at all. He doesn't move to kick me out. Though he could.

I take long walks, walks that last most of the day, even though each evening grows colder. I've stopped cooking for the two of us, scrounging in the pantry at night when I return, and Richard doesn't seem to mind. I don't know what he does when I'm not around. I walk all around the island, willing myself to absorb every detail of its rocky coast, every frond of seaweed that ripples beneath the water, knowing this cannot last, that it won't. At night I collapse into bed, and each morning I wonder if he will be there when I wake. And each morning he is.

$$=$$

On the third day, I wake to him in the kitchen. Clatter of pots and pans. There's a good smell, butter, and coffee in the pot. He's making omelets again, and there's already toast waiting on a plate. A peace offering. I get myself a cup of coffee and spread a piece of toast with jam, the jar leaving a sticky residue on my hand. I lick it off.

What's all this, I say, carefully.

Felt like it, he answers.

I watch him and bite into my toast. He hasn't cooked like this in weeks. He navigates the kitchen with ease, whisking and slicing, drizzling the beaten egg into the hot pan. Melted butter fills my mouth, and the taste of wild blueberries. In a few minutes a plate is set in front of me.

Voilà, he says.

Here he is, I think to myself. Just like that, in a full sentence. I don't know who the *he* is. It must be Richard. As if he's arrived somewhere, and I'm the one to greet him. The thought makes me feel strange, and then strong, like I might be the one with power now. He picks at his omelet while I have mine, and when I'm done he slides his over so I can finish it.

After, I do the dishes. It's cold today, and the hot water feels good on my bare hands. He's in the living room now, standing at his easel, though he hasn't started working. Yesterday he didn't paint at all. From here, I can see he's tired already, but he doesn't look unhappy about it, and I feel a sense of deep calm. The feeling seems to have no relation to my observation but arises at exactly the same time.

Christine, he says.

Yes.

I'm sorry, he says. For— He gestures, as if drawing an ellipse in the air.

I know, I say.

I think you should leave soon, he says. But. Before you go.

I look to him, listening.

That afternoon, we go out on his boat. There is a new gentleness between us, I think because I know I'm leaving, a gentleness that tips into a strange sweetness. He wants to teach me how to pilot, and he does, pointing out the ignition and the throttle. It's just like steering a car, he keeps saying, but I have trouble with it, I don't find it intuitive, and we move farther and farther from the shore as I learn. But I like the feeling of skimming over the waves, and the rumble of the engine when I push the throttle forward, and the way we're weightless, soaring over the ocean, even though when I look down I'm dizzied by how there's nothing but water underneath. Richard eggs me on, saying faster, faster, and the boat leaps when I rev the engine, and the wind fills our mouths as we shout over the waves. His eyes are sparkling. When I steer us west, toward the setting sun, his outline is fiery, haloed in light.

The sun is on the horizon by the time we decide to turn around. Long orange rays ripple across the water. Richard takes the helm and deftly steers us toward land again; I can just make out the shape of the house on its spit, extending over the sea. The lights are on, the wall of windows a bright rectangle against the dusk. We're cruising back when he cuts the engine.

Wait, he says. I want to go for a swim.

I don't think that's a good idea, I say.

I'll be fine, he says.

It's getting dark.

Just a short dip, he says.

Let's go tomorrow, I say, though I know I'm supposed to be leaving.

Come on, Christine.

In the dusk, I can't make out the color of his eyes, only the eerie pallor of his skin.

Just a swim. I want to see the bioluminescence.

I don't say anything.

Just for a minute or two, Christine. I'll be back before you know it.

I don't think it's a good idea, I say, but I relent, and he strips down in front of me, unselfconsciously, until he's standing in his underwear. Help me with this, will you, he says, and we take the metal ladder and hook it over the side of the boat. He hoists himself over the edge and climbs down, slipping into the water.

Even from here, I can see the sparks of light, the flashes of movement as the bioluminescence flickers against his arms and legs.

It's beautiful, I hear him say.

Then he begins to swim with purpose, stroking away from the boat, and I get a bad feeling.

Richard, I say, don't you fucking dare, *Richard*—

He's swimming hard and fast, and in the dimming light I'm already starting to lose sight of him in the water. I pull my sweater over my head and dive in. It's shockingly cold, so cold I nearly don't feel it, only the drag of the clothes I'm still wearing. And I can feel the hard, rushing current of the open ocean as I swim toward him, calling out his name when I lift my head for air.

Ten seconds, thirty—I don't know how long I'm swimming before I collide with him in the water, crashing into the warm bulk of him. I reach for him, blindly, and for a brief, terrifying moment we're struggling against each other in the water. Then I am completely submerged, all of it cold, all of it dark, except for those bright, iridescent sparks, waltzing in slow flashes beneath the water. Time seems to dilate, and a memory—absurd, slight—comes to me. A morning not long ago, here, on the island. Richard at the window, me reading, and I rise to get another cup of coffee. When I come back, my mug steaming, he says, Wait, and I turn to him. Come closer, he says, and I do. That smells good, he says, smiling slightly, before his face becomes grave, and then the memory is gone, and I'm exhaling for too long, air bubbles fizzing around my face, before there's a burst of white, all across my vision, and I surface, coughing, kicking hard, trying to keep us both afloat.

I have one hand on his wrist, and he's fighting me, trying to swim away. Then we really are fighting, flailing in the water, as I pull him toward me and he tries to wrench his arm out of my grip, swiping at me with his free hand.

Christine, he says hoarsely, his head barely above the waves. Let go of me.

When I release my grip I can see that his eyes are wet and bright. I'm treading water, watching him. Flashes of light pour off our bodies like tiny jewels.

Come back to the boat, I say, feeling desperate. Every second tugs us farther away from it, and I look back to see where we are now. Please, I say.

I reach for him but he moves backward, away from me. The water laps at his chin, his hollowed cheeks.

Christine, he says. Let me do this.

I don't want you to die, I say, my voice rising.

I'm already dying, Christine.

Water heaves into my mouth and I spit it out, coughing. I know I have to get back to the boat. I lunge for him, grabbing him by the wrist again. He tries to shake me off, but I hold fast.

Stop giving me this power, he says. You've given me too much already.

I can't—

I'm crying, and it surprises me.

I can't forgive you, I say. And you can't die until I do.

Christine, he says. He reaches for me with his free hand, takes hold of my face. His hand is so cold it feels like it's burning my skin. Either you let me ruin your life, or you get on with it. What will it be?

I turn away, jerking my head, but his grip is tight and he steers me back to face him. I'm crying hard now, and he's right, I've let him have this hold on me, I've let this story become the only story I know how to tell.

And I want so desperately for there to have been a reason but there will never be a reason, not one good enough that he can give me.

His hand falls from my face, though I still have hold of him, can feel the hard bones beneath his skin.

Richard, I say.

He looks at me. His eyes shining in the dark, his eyes like a raptor's, which I once believed could see everything.

I'm letting you go.

A flash of real fear moves through him. He nods, once.

And I turn from him, then. I release him.

I swim back to the boat, alone.

I climb the ladder in my wet clothes—heavy, I'm so heavy, and there's water all over the inside of the boat. Wind blows over the waves and I shiver. I turn the key in the ignition, push the throttle forward, and steer back toward the shore.

The house feels larger with just me in it. It's cold. I turn on the lights in the kitchen, punch the temperature buttons on the thermostat until I hear the boiler hiss to life. Then I strip, leaving my clothes in a pile on the floor, and take a shower. Steam rises from the hot water, from where it makes contact with the surface of my skin. I wash my hair once, twice, and I stand under the drumbeat of the water, examining my body carefully, taking note of the scrapes and cuts on my hands. After I am clean, I dress in new clothes. From the living room I can see the boats of the Coast Guard setting out, shining red and blue lights onto the water. I do not think they will find him, not at this hour.

I put the wet clothes from the boat in the wash. Some of the items, I realize, are his. The noise of the washing machine, and then the dryer, when I switch the load, is comforting to me. I decide to clean, sweeping the floors, wiping down surfaces. I find a can of glass cleaner in the linen closet and polish both mirrors until they shine, dully, in the dark. I re-oil and season the cast-iron, fold the laundry, and straighten the tall-backed chairs at the dining table. Then I walk through the rooms of the house.

The living room. There's a canvas on the easel. He'd been working on it earlier, and the surface is still wet. It's another seascape, still messy and abstract. It looks like the others, except for a small point of light in the sky. It could be a star, or it could be a planet. With the palms of both hands, I lift the painting off the easel and set it on the long bench in front of the windows to dry.

My room. My clothes half packed. My dresses swaying in the closet, like reeds in the wind. My computer, silver gray. The surface of the machine is cold to the touch.

His room. His altar of amber bottles. His bed, still made, without a single hair on the sheets.

Then I step into the other room, his old studio. Rows of his canvases lean against the walls. I'm looking for something, and I find it. A canvas, larger than the rest, stretched on wooden supports but not yet primed. There's a tub of gesso that I find, too, and a wide, long-handled brush.

I take the canvas into the room with the windows. Set it on the table, skimming my fingertips across its surface to feel the tooth of the weave. I pry open the lid of the gesso bucket with a flathead screwdriver and dip the brush in. Slowly, unhurriedly, I brush the gesso onto the canvas, recognizing the fluidity of it beneath my hands. I know it will dry quickly. I'll wait until it doesn't leave a mark when touched, and then I'll apply another coat.

ACKNOWLEDGMENTS

An ocean of gratitude to Meredith Kaffel Simonoff, my agent, who has been this book's best reader and dear advocate: It is an honor and a delight to get to think with you. Thank you to Marie Pantojan for your steadying, discerning edits; your boundless enthusiasm and empathy; and for making me feel so wonderfully at home at Little Random. Rowan Cope, my editor at Serpent's Tail: Thank you for the perceptive notes that have sharpened and brightened this book. Thank you also to Nora Gonzalez, Rebecca Gardner, and Will Roberts at the Gernert Company, and Rachel Clements of Abner Stein. Many hands go into the making of a book, and I am indebted to the fantastic team at Random House: Azraf Khan, Caitlin McKenna, Alison Rich, Andy Ward, Debbie Glasserman, Cara DuBois, Rebecca Berlant, Katie Zilberman, Jaylen Lopez, and Georgia Brainard.

Rachel Ake designed the genius, surprising cover which so perfectly captures the spirit of this book.

It was at the Bennington Writing Seminars where I rediscovered the love and practice of writing fiction, and I am so grateful for my instructors there: Monica Ferrell, Alice Mattison, Deirdre McNamer, and especially Stuart Nadler, who read the packets that would become *Discipline* and whose support from the very beginning of this project has been invaluable to me. Megan Galbraith invited me back as an alumni fellow, an experience I have treasured. Amina Mobley and Hannah Wilken: I love you and I am so glad Bennington brought us together.

In 2022, the Narode-Cleveland family invited me to spend some time on an island in Maine, which fully inspired the setting of the second part of this book. Thank you for the generosity of that gift, and for continuing to share the beauty of Maine's islands with me.

Thank you to: My fambly—Clare Mao, Rachel Kim, and Sophie Li. Santiago Sanchez, Alexandra Ashworth, Anna Meixler, Kara Clark. Everyone who let me sleep on their couch while I was commuting into the city these last two years. My upstate sangha community, the Third Jewel sitting group, and my therapist.

Thank you to my family.

Thank you to Ryan, for everything.

ABOUT THE AUTHOR

LARISSA PHAM is the author of the essay collection *Pop Song*, a finalist for the National Book Critics Circle John Leonard Prize. Her writing has appeared in *Granta*, *The Nation*, *The New York Times Book Review*, *Bookforum*, *Aperture*, and other publications. She holds an MFA in fiction from the Bennington Writing Seminars and is an assistant professor of writing at The New School. *Discipline* is her first novel.

larissapham.com
Instagram: @lrsphm

This book was set in Fournier, a typeface named for Pierre-Simon Fournier (1712–68), the youngest son of a French printing family. He started out engraving woodblocks and large capitals, then moved on to fonts of type. In 1736 he began his own foundry and made several important contributions in the field of type design; he is said to have cut 147 alphabets of his own creation. Fournier is probably best remembered as the designer of St. Augustine Ordinaire, a face that served as the model for the Monotype Corporation's Fournier, which was released in 1925.